The Wily Agent

Amar Bhushan joined the Indian Police Service in 1967 and was assigned to Madhya Pradesh. For seven years, he dealt with crime and law and order problems but remained a reluctant policeman. When the opportunity for working in intelligence organizations came, he grabbed it and never looked back till he retired as the chief of India's foremost technical intelligence agency. He began the second innings of his career by briefly serving in the BSF intelligence, State Special Branch and Intelligence Bureau and ended up with working in the Research and Analysis Wing for the next twenty-four years.

His last published work, *Escape to Nowhere*, remained on bestseller lists for eleven weeks. He lives with his wife and daughter in Bangalore but seldom misses an opportunity to visit his granddaughters in the US and his mother in Jasidih, a village in Jharkhand.

The Wily Agent

Amar Bhushan

HarperCollins *Publishers* India

First published in India by
HarperCollins *Publishers* in 2018

Building 10, Tower A, 4th Floor, DLF Cyber City, Phase II,
Gurugram Haryana – 122002, India
www.harpercollins.co.in

2 4 6 8 10 9 7 5 3 1

P-ISBN: 978-93-5277-903-1
E-ISBN: 978-93-5277-904-8

Typeset in 10.7/13.6 Cardo at
Manipal Digital Systems, Manipal

Printed and bound at
MicroPrints India, New Delhi

Acknowledgements

I owe this book entirely to Mr Vishal Bhardwaj, the extraordinary film-maker and Shantanu Ray Chaudhuri, editor at HarperCollins India. But for their prodigious indulgence, these stories would have remained buried in my dusty papers.

Vishal-ji, as I endearingly call him, was the first to read these stories. Since he found them readable and illustrative of what goes in undertaking covert intelligence operations, he persuaded Shantanu, who insists that I address him only by his first name, to go through the script. Shantanu did not have it easy to sell the idea of publishing spy tales that were a crossover between fiction and factual account of events to his colleagues. But his faith in his instincts finally paid off. Once the deck was cleared, he helped me with his invaluable suggestions to rewrite the original short stories and harnessed Shreya Dhawan's editing acumen to ensure that the narrative remained concise, free flowing and devoid of technical jargons. I would also like to thank Rea Mukherjee of HarperCollins India for her work in the final stages of the book.

My loving daughters also deserve a pat on their back – Keshani, for always providing a different perspective on how to script the events and Nilyanka, for making sure that I enjoy writing.

The Wily Agent

Dhaka, 1993

It was the worst of kal baishakhi, the 'season of doom'. Since early June, dusty squalls followed by thunderstorms and heavy rains had been lashing Dhaka and its adjoining areas, causing rivers to swell to dangerous levels and sweeping away settlements.

After a brief respite, the thunderstorms had returned to torment the city. Powerful gusts of wind, accompanied by long streaks of lightning, whipped trees and howled around buildings. A cloudburst threatened to tear the overcast sky apart and bring down torrential rains at any moment. Before it could get worse, Jeevnathan told his colleagues to rush home. He headed the unit of India's external intelligence agency in the Indian High Commission in Dhaka. At around 4.00 p.m., he too decided to leave as it had become ominously dark and had started drizzling. His secretary assisted him in securing the safe, almirahs and the room. Just as he was about to step out of his office, the internal phone on his desk rang. It was Sankar, who was in charge of the unit's telecommunication centre.

'Sir, I am in the process of receiving two coded cables marked most urgent. Should I bring them over to you this evening or send them to you tomorrow morning?' he asked.

'How much time will it take you to decode them?'

'An hour, sir.'

'I'll wait,' Jeev decided.

He asked his secretary to leave. He then walked over to the huge window in his office, drew aside the curtains and looked out. It had started pouring. He sat down on the sofa, took out a book from his briefcase on the phenomenon of migration of Muslims in Europe, recently sent to him by a friend in the US, and began reading. An hour and fifteen minutes later, Sankar brought him the deciphered text. The first cable was from Aseem Barua, the desk officer for Bangladesh at the Agency's headquarters. He had written:

> *'Expect a communication shortly from our unit in Wellington about a source (.) Would be grateful if you could meet him and convey your views on whether to exploit him for our future intelligence needs (.) Aroop is opposed to running this source (.) He believes that information provided by the source in the past has lacked credibility, been stale and of low quality (.)'*

Jeevnathan was at a loss as to why Barua would want his views when his boss Aroop Das considered the source to be worthless. Unless Barua wanted to witness the fireworks that would inevitably ensue from Jeev's communication to Das and vice versa. Ever since he had landed in Dhaka, Jeev's working relationship with Aroop, who controlled his station in his capacity as the desk officer of the Southeast Asia branch at headquarters, had been mostly confrontational. He found Aroop to be meddlesome and disliked his habit of rubbishing his operational proposals without providing any reason. Aroop had no qualms in making it known that he alone had the qualification to conceive, plan and execute operations. The others were simply there to follow his instructions. He also had a terrible habit of writing directly to junior members of Jeev's unit and advising them on how to run their sources. He stopped doing so only after Jeev threatened to move back to Delhi prematurely. But what frustrated Jeev most was Aroop's attempts to steal credit from his junior operatives and damage their reputations. Sadly, he had the eyes and ears of Rajamohan, the head of the Asia division, who could not see through his desk officer's deviousness—how he cheated his sources and inflated his indispensability. It was no wonder that Jeev avoided interacting with Aroop as far as possible, but whenever he had to, it usually ended in acrimonious exchanges.

The second cable was from Jeev's counterpart based in Wellington, New Zealand. He had written:

> *'We had recruited an official from the country where you are currently located (.) He was working here in his High Commission as a communication operator (.) His name is Shiraz (.) After completing his four-year tenure, he returned last month to your station where he is likely to be posted in the foreign office (.) While working with us, he regularly provided the gist of secret and top-secret communications but never shared original cables (.) He is greedy and clever and he knew that he was being paid for working for the Agency (.) He does not hesitate in accepting money since he has a tendency to live beyond his means (.) You may consider meeting him and then operating him if you find him suitable. I had an advantage*

over you in operating Shiraz since neither of us were under any kind of surveillance (.) Before his departure, I had proposed that he work for you, which he readily accepted (.) He would like to meet you for lunch at the Roll Express, which, he says, is less crowded and located in safer surroundings (.) I have asked him to give you a call on your embassy number and introduce himself as Sohrab's friend (.) Aroop does not trust this source (.) He believes that Shiraz is a cheat because he did not provide a single original cipher message (.) He is convinced that the source was taking me for a ride and that I was playing into his hands (.) He also suspects that Shiraz had contacted me at the behest of his country's intelligence service (.) I still maintain that he should not be dropped summarily without trying him out (.) He definitely has the potential to be a long-term asset (.)

Jeevnathan realized that he had a tough task at hand. Given his difficult relationship with Aroop, the stage was set for yet another round of harsh exchanges between the two. He deposited both cables in the safe, sealed it and walked down to the basement. It was deserted as all the employees of the High Commission had already left. He waited for a while in the car for the rain to ease. When that did not happen, he drove out, moving at a snail's pace against the gusting winds and torrential rains.

When he finally got home, half drenched from his sprint from the car to the front door, his wife Manini chided him for not waiting till the rain subsided. 'You have just recovered from a terrible spell of cold and cough. I don't know when you will learn your lesson.'

'I'll survive,' Jeev replied, smiling.

A cold was the least of his worries at the moment.

A week later, a man rang Jeevnathan on his office line, introducing himself as Sohrab's friend. Jeev guessed the caller was none other than Shiraz. But to make sure that he was indeed the right man, Jeev proposed that they meet the following day at the High Commission at 10.30 a.m.

'That is out of question. I cannot come to your office,' the caller insisted. 'The best that I can do is to meet you today at Roll Express at 1.45 p.m. They serve excellent salmon sandwiches and prawn fries. If you are a vegetarian, you will relish their vegetarian rolls, dosas and doifucha.'

'Since you seem to like this place and refuse to see me in my office, I will try to make it there,' Jeev replied, not wanting to lose the opportunity to meet the man and size him up. At the same time, he did not want to sound too eager to meet him. 'How will I recognize you?' he asked.

'I usually occupy the table in the far right corner of the restaurant, from where one can easily observe everything going on in the restaurant. A copper lamp, covered with a red shade, hangs over the table. On the wall to the right of the table is a painting of a bullock cart being driven by a poor farmer wearing a torn lungi.'

'I will be there along with a colleague.'

'But I was supposed to meet only you. Are you bringing him to ensure that I do not play foul with you?'

'You will know when you meet him,' Jeev said and disconnected.

He realized that Shiraz was a smart cookie and handling him wouldn't be easy.

He next rang up Arun, his deputy, and asked him to come to his office immediately. Of all the fifteen field operatives in the unit, Arun was Jeev's favourite and he involved him particularly in operations that required independent handling. What separated Arun from the herd was his ability to evade the watchers of the Bangladesh Special Branch and disarm even hostile sources with his sweet and persuasive talk.

As soon as Arun was seated in front of him, Jeev handed him both cables to read. Arun looked up thoughtfully after perusing them.

'I think we should exploit Shiraz, especially since there is no one on the unit's rolls who has this kind of access to correspondence between the Bangladeshi government and its missions abroad. Sir, if you agree, I can speak to one of my contacts to find out whether Shiraz has joined the foreign office,' he offered.

Jeev sensed that his prodigy saw the immense intelligence possibilities in working with Shiraz.

'He called me five minutes ago. I have agreed to meet him this afternoon. I suggest you accompany me. I have decided that you will be his handling officer,' Jeev said.

'Sir.'

'I will introduce you to the source under a cover name. I want to make sure you have deniability in case you are exposed. Do you have a name in mind that you can easily live with and not forget in a crisis situation?' Jeev enquired.

Arun thought for a moment. 'Sir, Kabir will be fine. It's my pet name and known only to my parents and close family members. It can also pass as both a Hindu and a Muslim name,' Arun suggested.

'Good. It will also be easy for me to remember. Meet me in my office at 1.00 p.m.,' Jeev said.

Jeevnathan used a back door to exit the High Commission and then walked to a nearby taxi stand. He kept observing his surroundings carefully to ensure that no one was following him. Arun a.k.a. Kabir trailed him discreetly at a distance. They got into separate taxis and took circuitous routes to reach Roll Express. The precautions were necessary to spot any watchers and avoid them; it was possible that the meeting was a trap and that the source had informed the Counter Espionage Unit (CEU) about his meeting with Jeevnathan.

At 1.55 p.m., Jeev and his deputy entered the restaurant together and saw a man occupying the corner table in the back. They walked towards him and Jeev greeted him as he sat down opposite him. Arun sat down next to the source without saying anything. The source didn't say anything either, simply nodding his head to acknowledge their arrival.

'I am sorry for the delay,' Jeev said.

'No problem. I got here only five minutes ago myself,' Shiraz responded. 'I did have some anxious moments when I tried to leave the office. My supervisor would not let me go for lunch till I finished deciphering the cables received since morning. Thankfully, I had taken the precaution of reserving the table in the morning so that we wouldn't have to wait or sit somewhere where we couldn't talk freely.' Shiraz looked around anxiously to spot anything suspicious.

'That was a sensible thing to do. Since you seem to be familiar with this restaurant, I suggest you order the food,' Jeev proposed.

As Shiraz read the menu card, Jeev took the opportunity to covertly size him up. The source was in his mid-thirties, with a dark brown complexion and slim build, and was probably no more than 5'7" tall. He sported a thick crop of black hair and his hollowed cheeks were covered with a neatly trimmed beard. Strangely, he appeared tense and very different from the man who had sounded so confident on the phone only a couple of hours ago.

'I have been keen to meet you. Sohrab spoke very highly of you as a person and an associate,' Jeev began to calm the source's nerves.

'Sir has always been very kind and generous,' the source replied. 'Mrs Sohrab was also very fond of my wife Rubeiya, who helped her buy the right kind of fish at a reasonable price, every week.'

'I am sure your family must have enjoyed living in Wellington. I am told it is a beautiful place.'

'Actually, I wanted to stay there for another year.' Shiraz seemed to relax a little. 'The ambassador liked my work immensely and even wrote to the foreign office requesting that they extend my tenure, but I decided to return to look after my old father.'

'And your mother?' Jeev asked.

'She died twenty years ago. I had to marry early, at the age of fifteen, and it was my father-in-law who financed the two years of my graduation and paid for the preparatory courses prior to my joining my present job,' he paused as the waiter came to take their order.

As soon as he left, Jeev decided to talk business.

'I don't know how frequently Sohrab met you in Wellington, but it may not be advisable for me to see you on a regular basis. You are handling a very sensitive desk and if you are seen with a senior Indian diplomat, it may arouse the suspicions of the Special Branch, which could impact your safety and career,' Jeev pointed out.

'You don't have to worry on that score. I can take care of myself, but I won't work with anyone other than you,' he stressed.

'Sohrab's case was different,' Jeev persisted. 'Both of you were working in New Zealand, where your activities were of no interest to its Security Intelligence Service. Here, many people know us. Seeing us meet frequently, they may begin questioning you and you may not be able to answer them satisfactorily.'

'I understand. That was why it took me a while to contact you. In fact, I had almost given up on working for the Agency while I was posted here. I even spoke to Rubeiya and to Sohrab about my predicament. But both advised me to give it a try and see how my relationship with you evolved over a period of six months before deciding whether or not to carry it forward.'

'You should not have called Sohrab on an open line. You never know, the National Security Intelligence may be monitoring the calls of all those working in the cipher unit. I hope your conversation went unrecorded. But it was a serious lapse on your part,' Jeev reprimanded him.

The source remained silent as he saw the waiter approaching with their food. Jeev politely declined eating anything, making the excuse that he was recovering from an upset stomach. He rarely had meals with sources in order to keep the discussions brief, pointed and less frivolous.

'I wish you had told me. I could have deferred the meeting,' Shiraz said.

'But I was keen to meet you,' Jeev said.

As Arun and the source tucked into the food, Jeev considered his next move.

'Let me introduce my colleague Kabir,' Jeev began. 'He will be your handling officer. He can pass easily as a Bangladeshi, and he speaks Bangla. I leave it to both of you to work out your modus operandi. However, I suggest that you meet at different locations and on different days and times, so that the Counter Espionage Unit of the NSI doesn't sniff out a pattern in your encounters. Kabir will convey my requirements to you, but that doesn't mean that I will not meet you,' he paused to observe Shiraz's reaction.

The latter looked up momentarily and then continued eating. Jeev realized that he was not briefing a novice.

'You should also avoid long intervals between meetings. Delayed reports will serve no purpose,' Jeev emphasized. 'But, at the same time, don't be rash. You know your security environment best. So, be patient, and only when you are absolutely confident, call Kabir to collect the messages. It may be a better idea to exchange documents and payments mostly through drop boxes.'

Totally focused on the food in front of him, Shiraz gave no indication of what he was thinking. Once he was finished eating, he finally looked up and requested Kabir to meet him four days hence at the Grand Mosque at 12.30 p.m.

'Do you have any specific place at the mosque in mind?' Kabir enquired, speaking for the first time.

'I suggest that you wait in the lawn to the right of the main entrance. I will meet you there. From there, we can move to a quieter place to talk business.'

Jeev wondered why Shiraz had not given his name so far and whether he wanted to be addressed by a different name to keep his Wellington identity concealed.

'How should we address you?' Jeev asked.

'Rehman will be fine since it is a common name in my country,' he promptly replied without batting an eyelid. It was obvious he did not want to be known as Shiraz in Bangladesh. It was equally obvious that Rehman was a hardened source, well aware of how to work as an espionage agent.

'Don't you want to know about your salary and the mode of payments?'

'I haven't even started providing you with reports. You should first read them and assess their quality. Only then will I be within my rights to fix the price tag.'

'Fine, but I will initially pay you three hundred dollars a month. However, there is no limit on the payment. It can always be hiked, depending on what you submit,' Jeev paused as the waiter came to clear the table. 'Thank you for meeting me and for agreeing to work with us,' he continued after the waiter left. 'I hope this is the beginning of a very productive relationship.'

'Are you a counsellor in the High Commission like Mr Sohrab?' Rehman suddenly enquired.

'No,' Jeev said. Before the source could probe further, Jeev stood up, shook hands with Rehman and left.

Seconds later, Kabir slipped a thousand takas into Rehman's pocket, which the latter accepted without any fuss. Then he went up to the reception desk to settle the bill and left. Rehman stayed on and ordered a cup of tea.

Kabir's first encounter with Rehman went smoothly. Both met at the entrance of the Grand Mosque at 12.30 p.m. The source was warm, friendly and relaxed. He guided Kabir to a roadside eatery in a crowded area where they discussed personal and professional matters, including the mechanics of their future meetings, while savouring fish curry and rice. Unlike a typical source, Rehman did not allow Kabir to pay the bill. He said jokingly that he had managed to save something from his stint in Wellington and would not mind spending some of them on hosting his new friend from India. After lunch, as Kabir was leaving the restaurant, Rehman handed him a folder.

That evening, Kabir reported to Jeev on his meeting with the source.

'Sir, the meeting went well. He spoke very fondly of his association with Sohrab, but sir, his opinion of you was not very flattering.' Kabir paused before continuing. 'He thought you were too stiff and businesslike and could not be a friend. He particularly disliked the manner in which you admonished him for talking to Sohrab.'

'I am not surprised. All my sources think alike. In fact, I thought that I was being too cordial,' Jeev remarked.

'Sir, he also said that for the risk that he was going to take, your offer of three hundred dollars was peanuts. He expects to be paid at least five hundred dollars a month.'

'Did he hand over a report?' Jeev asked.

'He has submitted nine cables. He gave them to me of his own accord. I didn't ask for them because it was our first meeting,' Kabir said and then passed Jeev a folder.

Jeev glanced cursorily through the cables before placing the folder on the side table.

'Anything else?'

'Sir, Rehman wants us to know that he will be able to collect and share only those messages that pass through his desk during his eight-hour shift. He will have no access to cables that are received either outside of his hours of duty or by his eleven other colleagues.'

'Did you ask him whether he could motivate his colleagues in the cipher section to work for us in the near future?' Jeev asked.

'Yes, sir, but he asked me to be patient. He claimed that everything was possible, but he would not subvert his colleagues or steal cables from them unless we committed to pay him a substantially higher amount,' Kabir said.

'I hope he is not exaggerating his potential. Try not to commit anything for the time being, but if he insists, tell him that everything will depend on what kind of information he provides,' Jeev cautioned.

'Sir.'

'Did you work out the operational drill?'

'Yes, sir. It was Rehman who selected our meeting places and the drop boxes and finalized the mode and frequency of our communication both during normal times and in emergencies. It almost seemed as if he was my running officer and I was his source. It is sometimes scary to hear him speak about how to defeat surveillance and what counter-measures I have to take when approaching the drop boxes. Sir, I have never met a source like him before.'

'I also feel that he is too smart for any operative's liking. Your skill in running a source will be fully tested this time,' Jeev remarked.

He then called in his secretary and dictated a cable for Aroop Das. He gave the details of his initial discussion with the source and Kabir's meeting with him and provided the highlights of the contents of the nine cables. He also mentioned that Rehman would probably not work for less than five hundred dollars a month as his salary.

A week later, Jeev received a biting communication from Aroop.

'*I read your cable. Two hundred and fifty dollars is the maximum that can be sanctioned for the trash that the source has provided. I am not interested in learning about political developments in other countries from him. You are a senior officer and should have known better.*'

Jeev seethed with anger and wasted no time in sending a strong rejoinder.

'*Rehman is a gold mine. It will be a mistake to lose him due to our petty squabbles. This is his first set of messages. Who knows what he will bring to us in the future? I cannot understand this constraint of money. We seldom blink an eyelid in sanctioning huge sums to sustain bogus operations. As for my seniority, I am not sure if twenty-two years of service is enough for being called "senior" since I am still being dictated to by all and sundry. Please have a fresh look at this prospect.*'

Jeev waited for a venomous response, but it did not arrive, Barua, however, called. He confided that Aroop had been furious after reading Jeev's reply, but had decided against sending a scathing response for reasons best known to him. He had, however, claimed that he had shown the cable to Rajamohan who, according to him, was upset and had assured Aroop that he would pull up Jeev for his behaviour.

'Aroop is lying as usual,' Jeev said. 'Rajamohan spoke to me only this morning seeking my advice on an operational matter concerning one of his assets, but he mentioned nothing about my cable.'

There was silence for a few seconds.

'Sir, Aroop is adamant on sanctioning only two hundred and fifty dollars a month to Rehman and not a penny more. Since he knows that you will protest, he has taken Mr Rajamohan's approval on file before he conveys the decision to you,' Barua updated him.

'I don't know why Rajamohan listens to him. Tell Aroop that you spoke to me and I want him to know that I will continue to pay three hundred dollars a month to the source. It's for him to decide whether he reimburses the bill in full or in installments. I cannot let this operation suffer because of him.'

'Sir, he has also decided to review the operation after three months. After that he will let you know whether the source needs to be dropped or maintained on a nominal sum.'

'Let him do what he does best, which is conspiring. Reviewing the work of officers and assets objectively has never been his forte,' Jeev said in disgust and hung up.

For the next three months Rehman regularly submitted secret and top-secret cables to Kabir. In every meeting he asked for an increase in his salary, claiming that he was putting his life at stake, and in return receiving a sum that was not even enough to buy groceries for a week.

'Sir, Rehman continues to push for an increase in his salary. This time, he threatened to stop working if it wasn't hiked to seven hundred and fifty dollars immediately,' Kabir briefed Jeev on his latest meeting with the source.

'And what did you say?' Jeev asked.

'I told him that every effort was being made to meet his financial requirements, but he dismissed my reassurances. He said that unlike you, Sohrab wielded significant clout with officers at headquarters and never had any problems in obtaining funds for his assets. He thinks that because of your domineering attitude you cannot get officers at headquarters to support you. He called you a lone wolf and is not sure whether his association with us can last more than a year.'

'I guess he's right,' Jeev said, smiling. 'For now, try and pacify him as best you can.'

However, this time Jeev took Rehman's threat a little more seriously and wrote a more measured and persuasive note to Aroop, underlining the potential of the source, his monetary expectations and how he proposed to utilize him.

Aroop refused to even acknowledge the communication.

But once again, Barua called. 'Sir, he showed me your letter, but he is neither going to act on it nor reply.'

'Has he shown it to Rajamohan?' Jeev enquired.

'No, sir.'

'Is he in the habit of not putting up papers received from the field if they are not to his liking?'

'Yes, sir. Actually, you should have sent your requirement via a cable, as all cables are seen by Rajamohan and the Chief.'

'I see. And what has he done with the quarterly review of Rehman's performance?' Jeev enquired.

'Usually the branch carries out the review and sends the draft to him. But in this case, Aroop himself reviewed the output of the source and has assessed his performance as below par. He has dubbed almost all his reports as insipid, sketchy and routine. We sent you his remarks yesterday,' Barua said.

'Thanks. I will read his report when it comes, but tell me the gist of what he has written.'

'Let me read out the relevant portions from the original file,' Barua said and began reading:

> *'Evidently Rehman has not been properly briefed on our priorities. That is why he is offering vague and generalized reports on countries that are of no concern to us. If the source is not squeezed hard in the beginning, he will not make any effort to procure hard intelligence in the security and strategic areas. There will be no increase in his salary till the next review.'*

'Aroop is merely repeating himself,' Jeev said. 'He has conveniently ignored the fact that Rehman has also provided information on Dhaka's recent interest in the acquisition of military hardware from Islamabad, the proposed visit of the Bangladesh Army chief to Pakistan and how Dhaka plans to corner India on its repeated allegations that Bangladesh is sponsoring insurgency from its soil.'

'Sir, in our internal discussions prior to his writing the review, I reminded him of these very points, but he brushed them aside,' Barua confided.

'You have done what you could. You can't chisel sand.'

Jeev was caught in a dilemma. He had to find a way to keep Rehman motivated to continue providing reports without being distracted by his insatiable greed for money, and to make Aroop understand that there was enormous benefit in retaining the source even at a high cost. He decided he would first tackle the source and handle Aroop later and asked Kabir to set up a meeting with the source sometime during the following week.

The meeting turned out to be a nightmare. At 1.30 p.m., Kabir took Jeev to the designated meeting place, a restaurant in downtown Dhaka. The place was Rehman's choice; he had told Kabir that it was famous for its kebab and keema roti, cooked by chefs who traced their culinary expertise to their forefathers who had served in the court of Nawab Siraj-ud-Daulah. It was located in a dingy and crowded lane some hundred and twenty metres away from the main road. It was tiny, the smell of food and sweat was overwhelming, and it was so packed that Jeev had to turn and twist his way through, only to find there was no table available. The walls were painted a garish green, the curtains were filthy and the tables were covered with cheap printed plastic sheets. Several people were standing outside, waiting impatiently for a table, and those inside were mobbing the lone man who was taking orders, receiving payments and directing guests to tables. Suffocated, Jeev decided to leave after fifteen minutes, chiding Kabir for selecting such a dreadful place for a source meeting.

'Sir, I knew you wouldn't like it. I had the same reaction when he brought me to reconnoitre the place. I repeatedly told him to shift the venue to Lemon Grass, but he was insistent. He said that it was safer to discuss business in a crowded place rather than in a quieter restaurant in a posh locality,' Kabir clarified.

'Rubbish. How can one discuss anything in this chaos?' Jeev asked in annoyance as he shouldered his way out.

Both waited outside the restaurant for another half hour, but there was no sign of Rehman. Fed up, Jeev told Kabir they were leaving.

'Sir, I'm surprised Rehman didn't show. This is the first ever miss by him; he usually keeps his appointments and if for some reason he can't, he has always let me know in advance,' Kabir said, trying to soothe the ruffled feathers of his boss as they walked towards the main road.

Jeev said nothing.

'Sir, it is possible that he was caught by the CEU watchers,' Kabir continued.

'Let's not flirt with nightmares,' Jeev snapped. 'For all you know, he may have just forgotten.'

'Sir, there is definitely something wrong. He may appear to be very brave, but he is actually timid. He keeps talking about his contacts in the NSI and Special Branch, probably to reassure himself that nothing will happen to him. He is the kind of person who will crack easily and spill everything the moment he is tackled hard.'

By now they had reached the main road and Jeev was looking for a rickshaw. Suddenly, he saw Rehman. He was right behind Kabir. He tapped Kabir on his right shoulder and quickly slipped a piece of paper into his back pocket. Before Jeev could question him, the source was gone. Kabir pulled out the typed message and read it aloud to Jeev:

> *'Our meetings will have to be brief in future. I suspect I am being followed by CEU watchers, but I may be wrong. I will, however, continue to fill the drop boxes. Bring my enhanced salary when we meet next.'*

'He is playing games with us. No one is watching him,' Jeev said. 'This note is his way of reminding us that we need him more than he needs us and that we therefore have to follow his dictates. I suggest you skip one or two meetings deliberately and when you see him next, tell him that you will choose the venue for meeting in future.'

Strangely, there was no word from Rehman for the next two months, but he kept filling the drop boxes with cables and collecting his salary from them. Then, one day at 4.30 a.m., he called Kabir.

'Sorry to wake you so early, but I'm on the night shift and took the opportunity to call you,' he began. 'I don't have much time, so I'll keep this short. If it is convenient for your boss, we can dine at Jharna Grill in the Sonargaon Hotel on Friday at 8.30 p.m. They serve excellent authentic Bangladeshi seafood.'

'I'll speak to my boss and confirm.'

'Okay,' Rehman said and hung up.

Kabir tried to sleep but could not. Something about the call bothered him. The timing, date and place of the meeting were suspicious. In the past, the source had always met him during lunch hours at crowded eating joints and that too only on working days. Jharna Grill, on the other hand, was not only expensive but also exclusive. Was it possible that the CEU had discovered Rehman's involvement in espionage, taken him into custody for interrogation and had then forced him to set up the dinner to find out who his handlers were? But if that were so, how was it that he had continued to deliver cables to the drop boxes? Could they have been doctored?

When he shared his fears with Jeev, the latter agreed that while anything was possible, he would nonetheless not dump the source without first going to Jharna Grill.

'Maybe for a change he wants to eat in decent surroundings at my cost. I think we should bite the bait. As a precaution, tell him that we will be going there only to enjoy the food. There will be no discussion about work, no documents will be exchanged and no payments will be made,' he said.

Kabir later put a note conveying Jeev's directions in drop box 4.

The meeting at Jharna Grill never materialized. At 8.15 p.m. on Friday, Jeev entered the restaurant and sat at a table facing the entrance. He told the waiter that he was expecting a friend and ordered an onion soup and prawn bites to bide the time. But neither Rehman nor Kabir turned up. Finally, at 9.30 p.m., he paid the bill and left.

When he reached home, Manini was having her dinner. He joined her at the dining table and served himself some vegetables and salad.

'Weren't you supposed to have dinner with your source or whoever he or she may be?'

'The man did not turn up,' Jeev said.

After dinner, he sat in the living room to watch the news while Manini went to instruct the servants to shut the windows and doors as a storm had begun, lashing the trees in the compound, and a downpour seemed imminent. Suddenly, she heard someone knocking on the front door. She went to answer it and found Kabir standing there. She invited him in and directed him to the visitors' room. Jeev joined him there after a few minutes.

'What happened? Why didn't you come to the restaurant?' Jeev demanded as they settled down.

'I am sorry, sir. Rehman caught me in the lobby of the hotel as I was heading to the restaurant. He seemed flustered and asked me to follow him discreetly. When we got to the parking lot, he finally told me that at the last moment, he had learnt from a friend that Jharna Grill was commonly used by foreign handlers to meet sources, and it was on the CEU watchers' radar. I wanted to go back inside to inform you, but Rehman insisted on leaving the hotel immediately. We ended up at a small eatery called Star,' Kabir explained.

'If he knew that the place was unsafe, why did he choose the hotel to meet us in the first place?'

'He said that he thought he'd take a chance and went to reconnoitre the restaurant before we arrived. However, when he spotted a couple of suspicious-looking men, he decided that it wasn't safe for us to meet there and waited outside the hotel to whisk us away. But he must have missed you. When he didn't see us, he went inside, where I met him,' Kabir said.

'This is all nothing but his theatrics. He is creating this surveillance scare to make us believe that he is endangering his life for us and that is why he needs to be paid more.'

Kabir remained silent.

'What did he have to say about his long absence?' Jeev asked.

'His mother-in-law died and he had to leave for the village to arrange for the funeral services.'

'He is lying. It doesn't take several weeks to arrange and attend a funeral service. Besides, if he really did leave town, he wouldn't have been filling the drop boxes with cables every week,' Jeev pointed out.

'I am sorry, sir, that didn't occur to me. In fact, I sympathized with him,' Kabir said, mortified.

'Clever sources often try to invoke pity to extract the handler's indulgence. Avoid reacting to his personal problems as best as you can. Anyway, did you tell him that I was waiting at the Jharna Grill?'

'Yes, sir. He said that he was very keen to meet you, but not at the cost of your safety. He also wanted to know why his salary had not been hiked and hinted that he might stop working for us. He also had some hot news, which he was keen to hand over to you personally. He asked me to check if a meeting on Friday at 12.30 p.m. at Haji Biryani would suit you,' Kabir said.

'That's fine with me, but I doubt he will make it,' Jeev said. 'Where is the hot news that he claims to have gathered?'

'Sir, he was initially hesitant to give it to me but later changed his mind.'

Jeev went through the copies of the cables that Kabir handed to him. They were indeed hot, covering Dhaka's directions to its ambassadors in Saudi Arabia and China about the Bangladeshi president's forthcoming visit to those countries.

'I knew he would come good one day,' Jeev said, almost to himself. 'How did you get here?' he then asked.

'I took a three-wheeler, sir.'

'Let me drop you home,' Jeev offered.

'Sir, please don't worry. The storm has already subsided and it is unlikely to rain. It's just a fifteen-minute walk to my house.'

'It's not safe to walk alone this late at night,' Jeev insisted as he picked up the car keys from the sideboard.

He drove Kabir to his residence, followed throughout by two watchers on a motorbike.

By the time Jeev returned home, it was 12.30 a.m. Manini reminded him that he had to go to the airport to receive his eldest daughter Maitri at 7.30 in the morning.

Kabir desperately hoped that Rehman would show up and not let him down. To make sure that there were no last-minute changes in the venue or the date of the meeting, he left his house at 5.00 a.m. to check drop box 7. In it he found an envelope containing three cables. Then, soon after Kabir returned home, Rehman called him to confirm that 'the event was on'. At noon, Kabir drove Jeev to Haji Biryani, parked his diplomatic car some distance away and walked with Jeev to the restaurant. Inside, the aroma of food was irresistible. Once seated, Jeev began glancing through the menu, wondering whether Rehman would bother to show up this time. He didn't have long to wait to find out. Barely five minutes later, Rehman approached, greeted them and sat down.

'I have some urgent matters to discuss with you,' he began in a low voice. 'But I can't talk here in such raucous surroundings. Why don't both of you come to my home for dinner tonight? My wife would be happy to prepare an excellent meal for you.'

Jeev looked at him speculatively before responding. 'Thanks, but I take only fruit and soup at night.'

Rehman merely nodded. Kabir passed him an envelope containing his salary, which the source quickly pocketed. He then extracted an envelope from a leather pouch, handed it to Kabir and left. He stopped briefly at the sales desk, picked up his takeaway order and exited.

Jeev took the envelope from Kabir and opened it. It contained five messages and a note giving directions to Rehman's residence as well as a sketch of the layout of his house. Jeev and his deputy stayed on and had biryani and kebab, essentially to ensure that anyone watching them would not take it amiss if they left the restaurant without have a meal.

'Sir, this man is definitely up to some mischief. He can come here with reports and wait to collect his food, but insists on discussing important matters only in his home. He is probably laying a trap for us,' Kabir said as the waiter left after clearing the table.

'You may be right. He's also stretching his luck a bit too far. But I'm willing to give him the benefit of the doubt this time. Besides, Haji Biryani is actually not the ideal place to discuss issues of payments and the quality of his reports,' Jeev said as he looked around the small and crowded eatery.

Back in the office, Jeev continued to ponder over the advisability of going to Rehman's house, especially when the source himself suspected that he was under surveillance. Kabir tried his best to persuade Jeev to abandon the visit, but the latter finally decided that he would take the chance. There were many matters weighing on his mind that he wanted to tell the source at the earliest.

'I have to meet him and do some tough talking,' he explained. 'He has so far been collecting cables indiscriminately without assessing their usability. Aroop is not totally wrong when he says that most of his cables are not worth a dime. Rehman needs to be clearly told that any increase in his salary will depend on the quality and not the volume of his information.'

'Sir, you can do the same thing at a safer and quieter restaurant,' Kabir countered politely.

But Jeev viewed the situation differently. 'It's taken nearly four months for Rehman to finally find the time to meet me face to face. I cannot let this opportunity go. And he needs to course correct his modus operandi before his next quarterly review. For that, I have to clearly brief him on our short, middle and long-term priorities. I cannot postpone meeting him any further.'

'Sir, maybe I can go and meet him and bring up these points on your behalf?'

'No, let me play the tough cop. I am also thinking of going alone to meet him,' Jeev said.

Kabir was aghast. 'Sir, that is out of the question. You never know, he may be laying a trap and it would be suicidal for you, the head of the Agency's unit, to walk into it knowingly,' he warned. 'It will be impossible for me to retrieve the situation if you get caught.'

'I don't think that will happen. But if you insist, I can take you along,' Jeev said. 'You can cover the house while we talk. If you notice anything unusual, call on Rehman's number to say that the tiger is on the prowl. If you look at the layout of the house provided by the source, you will notice that there is a courtyard at the back, which has a door that opens out to a lane. As a precaution, park your car in this lane; it merges with a street that runs parallel to the main road, so we can use it to escape.'

'But, sir, if I sit in the car, I will not be able to cover the front door and you may not have time to come out,' Kabir argued.

'Don't worry. One knock by the surveillance team on the front door and I will be out from the rear door in a flash. I will also ask Rehman to post someone outside the front door to monitor any suspicious activity. If we agree on this plan, we move separately at 7.30 p.m. and reach his house around 8.00 p.m.,' Jeev said.

Kabir agreed reluctantly, convinced that his boss was taking an undue risk.

A taxi dropped Jeevnathan off on the service road near Rehman's home. From there, he walked towards the source's house, which was located at the far end of an alley. The area was dimly lit and bustling with children and their yelling parents. On reaching the house, Jeev rang the bell. Rehman himself opened the door. He greeted him and led him inside to the living room. Jeev sat down on a sofa, which was covered neatly with an imported printed bed sheet. He looked around. Most of the furniture was imported, although it wasn't of the expensive kind. Three coloured glass lamps hung from the ceiling and a photograph of a lady, probably Rehman's mother, against the backdrop of Mecca adorned one of the walls. Rehman told him that his father had bought the house many years ago, but it was his wife who had changed it completely and made it into a home.

Within a few minutes, the room was filled with all of Rehman's family members. One by one, the source introduced Jeev to his wife Rubeiya, his five-year-old son Jamal, his younger brother Qasim and his father. Jeev found everyone to be curious but respectful. He had no idea what Rehman had told his family about the nature of their relationship and whether he had kept them in confidence about his new name. He decided to play it safe and avoided addressing him as 'Rehman' during the entire conversation. Qasim brought in refreshments, which Jeev politely declined, saying that he had an upset stomach. Jamal and Qasim, huddled together near the doorway, kept gazing at him. Rubeiya enquired about his wife and talked nostalgically about her stay in New Zealand. Unlike her husband, she was comfortable speaking in English. She also appeared to be well aware of local political developments. After a few minutes, Rehman told his family members that he needed to speak to Jeev privately and they all left after politely bidding him farewell. The last to leave was his father who lingered a little longer, recalling his past association with Indian leaders during the freedom movement.

'Why do you think you are being tailed?' Jeev enquired as soon as they were alone.

'I have no evidence, but I get the feeling that I am being watched. Whenever I call home from the office, I hear a screeching noise in the beginning, followed by a jumble of voices. I think my calls are being monitored,' Rehman said.

'If that is your worry, I will send you a device. Connect it to your phone. It will block any unwanted listeners and help you identify suspect callers.'

'So far, no one has questioned me. Maybe I'm reading too much into the increased presence of security officers near my office. But sometimes I do notice the same faces around me.'

'What if the NSI goons barge into the room right now and catch us together?' Jeev asked.

'Qasim is outside, keeping an eye out for any suspicious activity.'

'Good. I was going to tell you to have someone keep watch.'

'But why are you worried? You are a diplomat and nothing will happen to you. Where is Mr Kabir? I thought you would bring him along as well.'

'He had to go to Calcutta to take care of some urgent personal business. He should be back in two days. You told us that you had some important matters to discuss. What is it?' Jeev asked, coming straight to the point.

Rehman nodded and left the room, returning shortly with an envelope.

'This contains seven cables. I had them lifted from the foreign minister's office. They relate to your country and Pakistan,' he said.

'Are these the originals?' Jeev enquired.

'Yes.'

'Why didn't you photocopy them? The dealing hands may ask for an investigation if the originals are found to be missing.'

'Photocopying was not possible. The copier room is always busy. But you can photocopy them and return the originals to me. I will have them restored to the concerned files,' Rehman said.

'Okay, but how did you manage to access these documents? Someone must have helped you to lift them.'

'Yes. I will introduce him to you shortly.'

'Does he know the end user of these reports?'

'No. His interest is only in money. He can produce anything that you need, but for a price.'

'Let him submit a few more reports. We can decide in due course how much to pay to keep him happy. Meanwhile, please try to win over your colleagues who handle the traffic relating to Pakistan and China.'

'I can try, but don't give up on the foreign office contact. You will realize his value when you meet him. You don't know how much money and effort I had to put in to make him steal those papers. If you find them useful, let me know. I have a general idea of your area of interest, but if you can be a little more specific, it will be easier for him to access them on a regular basis,' Rehman said.

'It is better that you handle him till I have some feedback from headquarters on the authenticity and worth of his information.'

'Are you satisfied with my work?' Rehman asked. 'I haven't heard a word of appreciation from you for my reports nor I have been rewarded for all the information I have provided on exchanges between Dhaka and Delhi on a number of important issues.'

'I know that the feedback on your work is long overdue. Actually, I recently received a detailed assessment of your output from headquarters. I deliberately did not pass it on to you because it rates your performance as average,' Jeev lied. 'I suggest you revert to the earlier practice of sending all cables that you can lay your hands on. Headquarters is of the view that what you pick and choose is not always what we are looking for. I know you are doing it on our advice, but from now onwards, please hand over as many cables as possible.'

'You have no idea of the risk that I am taking to submit these cables. I can't do more under the circumstances. If you are not happy with my work, tell me. I will stop meeting Mr Kabir.'

'There is no need to get upset,' Jeev responded calmly to prevent the situation from spinning out of control. 'It is natural that our expectations will rise sky-high when we come across a source of your calibre. We do not want to lose you, and we are very concerned about your security. You must be extra careful, particularly when you visit the drop boxes and collect papers and copy them.'

'This is not the first time that I am taking such risks,' Rehman said.

'I don't dispute that. But I feel it is my duty to caution you against being too sure of yourself.'

'What is it that you find so objectionable about the way I operate? If you think I am a nut and will expose you, why don't you just drop me? I think that all this concern about my safety is just an excuse to pay me less and force me to drop out.' Rehman looked genuinely aggrieved.

'Try to be reasonable. We are here to work together and not to find fault with each other. I came simply to suggest that you need to cut down on your personal meetings with Kabir ... maybe restrict them to once a month. I am told that you call Kabir from your personal phone whenever there is something to share on an urgent basis. You should never do that because the NSI may be tapping both yours and Kabir's phones. I have also noticed that of late you prefer meeting in four- or five-star restaurants. This needs to stop, because such places usually attract the attention of surveillance units. It is always safer to meet in teashops or kiosks in crowded areas to pass on your papers and receive payments. But if you feel that I have no business advising you on your modus operandi, don't blame me if you run into trouble.'

'All this is fine, but what you are paying me for my efforts is negligible. I have shared so much, but you seem reluctant to loosen your purse strings. I had to pay five hundred dollars to my contact in the foreign office. I don't know whether you will reimburse it. You probably think that you have to pay only enough to keep me alive. It can't go on like this forever,' he warned.

'I have already recommended a substantial hike in your salary,' Jeev lied and handed him a packet containing eight hundred dollars and a Gadwal silk sari for his wife.

Rehman accepted the packet without saying anything.

'Would you not like to open it and see what is inside?'

The source took out the dollars, counted them and grinned.

'I must leave now,' Jeev said and stood up.

Rehman requested him to wait for just a moment, quickly left the room and returned with Rubeiya.

'Thank you for the sari, it's beautiful,' she said, smiling.

'My wife selected it; she'll be pleased to know that you liked it.'

'I have just made some hilish pulav. You must take some home with you.'

'Thank you, but I must decline. We are strict vegetarians,' Jeev responded, smiling apologetically. 'And now I really must leave.'

Rehman escorted him out.

Jeev circled around to the lane that ran behind Rehman's house, where Kabir had parked his car. He found him waiting anxiously. Visibly relieved to see his boss return safely, he wasted no time in starting the car and driving off.

'Sir, I didn't notice any suspicious movement around Rehman's house. In fact, I'm fairly certain that Rehman faces no threat of arrest nor is he under any kind of watch,' Kabir reported.

Jeev merely nodded.

'Sir, how did the meeting go?'

'It wasn't easy. Rehman's problem is that he is wily and clever by half,' Jeev remarked.

Kabir couldn't agree more. The rest of the drive passed in silence. Kabir dropped Jeev off on the main road near his house.

As Jeev walked towards his residence, two watchers followed him clumsily.

After a quiet dinner, he retired to his bedroom and went through the documents handed over by Rehman. The material was explosive. Manini joined him after some time.

'Did your friend's wife like the sari?' she enquired as Jeev put the cables in the drawer of the side table and switched off his bedside lamp.

'She liked it immensely and thanked you for sending it.'

'I'm sure she will look stunning in it,' she said mischievously.

Jeev wisely avoided falling into her trap. 'She wanted to send hilish pulav for you, but I said you are vegetarian,' he said instead.

'Why did you lie? You know that I love fish.'

'I didn't want to encourage her to be social,' Jeev said and rolled on to his side, pulling the sheet up over himself.

The originals that Rehman's friend in the foreign office had submitted were a gold mine. They were top-secret exchanges between Dhaka, Islamabad and Beijing on critical strategic, military and commercial issues. One of the cables listed talking points for the heads of missions to counter the allegations by India that the Bangladesh Army was actively involved in sheltering insurgents and terrorists.

Jeev sent Aroop the gist of the cables and the highlights of his meeting with the source and followed this up by dispatching all seven reports. As expected, Aroop did not reply. But Barua called. He said that he had been instructed by his boss to inform Jeev that the salary of two hundred and fifty dollars would not be enhanced.

'I am not surprised, but I did not know he was so crazy. Is he totally blind that he cannot see the huge potential of this source? Has he shown my cable and the latest set of top-secret reports provided by the source to Rajamohan?' Jeev asked.

'I don't think he has. But he has used the information in reports to the government,' Barua confided.

'Does he take Rajamohan's consent before turning down proposals to hike the salary of sources?'

'No, sir.'

'I guess I will have to bypass him and write to Rajamohan to handle this operation directly,' Jeev remarked.

'Sir, he may not agree,' Barua opined. 'He depends heavily on Aroop. In any case, he has been poisoned against you and may not look at your proposal objectively.'

'Do you think so?' Jeev asked.

'Yes, sir. Last week Aroop submitted a note to Rajamohan, complaining about your habit of unilaterally rewarding your sources and hiking their salary without approval from headquarters. He stated that you did not care about procedures and always forced headquarters' hand in sanctioning all such payments retrospectively. He further wrote that you were following the same strategy in Rehman's case even though it was evident that the source was merely biding his time before exposing you,' Barua informed him.

'And what did Rajamohan say?'

'He signed the note and returned it,' Barua replied.

'Irrespective of what Aroop and his boss feel, I will continue paying whatever the source asks for. I can't let national security interests suffer because of one petty and stubborn officer. I know I sound like the ultimate conscience keeper, but I don't give a damn,' Jeev declared before hanging up.

For the next four months, Rehman was at his productive best. He passed on dozens of classified cables and regularly met Kabir. Jeev was able to pay him six hundred and fifty dollars a month following an in-house manipulation of service funds. However, there was no let up in the greed of the source for more. In one meeting with Kabir, Rehman demanded a thousand dollars to bribe his way through to the Pakistan desk. Since Jeev did not want to lose the opportunity, he arranged for the payment without obtaining approval from headquarters and sent the bill to Aroop after posting the expenditure under a different operation for reimbursement.

Rehman's plan worked out perfectly. He was first moved to the Southeast Asia desk and a month later, he was shifted to the Pakistan desk.

The change of desk resulted in a quantum jump in the quality of Rehman's inputs. In the very first consignment of six cables, he submitted reports on Dhaka's concern over the finances provided by Pakistan's Inter-Services Intelligence to politicians and to train Kashmiri militants in Bangladesh. This was followed by the submission of critical information on security, economic and strategic matters. The source even started forwarding original cables to allay all suspicions about his bona fides. Within two weeks, approvals for all ad hoc payments billed so far by Jeev were received. The source's salary was also raised to five hundred dollars, although that was still a hundred and fifty dollars short of what Jeev had been paying. A week later, when Rajamohan called to get an update on another operation, Jeev raised the issue of Rehman's salary. Within a few days, the full amount of six hundred and fifty dollars was sanctioned as Rehman's salary and all his arrears cleared. Finally, everything seemed to be falling into place.

But Jeev was still apprehensive, for his luck rarely lasted beyond a few months.

It was a traumatic day for Kabir. He went for his daily morning walk, had an early breakfast and left for the airport to drop off his son who had come to Dhaka to spend his mid-term vacation. From there, he proceeded straight to drop boxes 3 and 5, which were to be cleared around 11.30 a.m. as per the schedule. Surprisingly, both were empty. The typed sheet listing out points for the source to cover, which Kabir had left a week ago, was still in drop box 5, untouched. Apparently, the source had not visited these drop boxes. A little worried, Kabir rang up the source from a public booth on a previously assigned number, but there was no response. Then he called a contact in the telephone exchange, who told him that the number was no longer in service. In a panic, Kabir tried an emergency number, which was of a distant cousin of the source. The cousin told Kabir that he had not seen Rehman for quite some time.

With no prospect of contacting the source, Kabir rushed to the office and broke the news to Jeev.

'I suggest you go to his house discreetly tonight and find out what has happened,' Jeev said.

'Sir, do you think it is advisable to go alone under these circumstances?' Kabir asked.

'We have no choice. One of us has to go.'

'Okay, sir. I will ask one of my local contacts to position himself in the area and keep a watch on all suspicious movements. He will inform you in case I am lifted by the CEU.'

'That situation will not arise,' Jeev reassured him. 'And don't forget to carry some money. It may come in handy in bribing your way out of tricky circumstances.'

At 9.30 that night, an anxious Kabir rang the doorbell of Rehman's house. Rubeiya opened the door and was surprised to see Kabir and his wife standing there. She greeted them warmly and invited them in.

'I'm afraid my husband won't be able to join us. He has a terrible viral infection and has been lying sick for the past two weeks. He hasn't even been able to go to the office this week,' Rubeiya said apologetically.

Kabir felt an immense wave of relief wash over him. Rehman was not compromised.

'May I see him for a few minutes?' Kabir asked, feigning concern.

'Of course,' Rubeiya said and led Kabir to their bedroom. She left him there and returned to keep Kabir's wife company.

Rehman was sitting in a cane chair, looking frail.

'What a surprise! I knew you would be restless to see me but to this extent?' the source said feebly, smiling. 'Why don't you pull up that chair?' He paused as Kabir sat down in the chair indicated. 'Rubeiya must have told you that I've been unwell. Initially, I was able to go to the office. In fact, last Tuesday evening I attempted to drop off a report on my way back home from work, but there were too many people loitering near drop box 2 in Dhanmandi Lake Park. The next day, I attempted to deposit the cables during my lunch break, but once again I was unable to, this time because I thought watchers were following me.' He paused again to catch his breath. 'Since then, I have not been able to move from the house. From now on, I will use drop boxes 5 and 9 most of the time.'

'I hope you are not confusing watchers with regular walkers in the park,' Kabir ventured.

'No. I know for sure that they were from the Special Branch,' Rehman asserted.

'In that case we can stop meeting for a few weeks. On my way to your house, I kept a careful lookout to see if I was being followed. But there was no one. If you are under active surveillance, why wouldn't the CEU watch over your house?'

'I really don't know,' Rehman said.

Kabir decided to drop the topic as Rehman was beginning to look exhausted. Their conversation moved to more general matters. Inevitably, Rehman brought up Jeev's unfriendly attitude, his miserliness and his inability to make the best use of Rehman's operational reach. Kabir merely listened, wisely deciding against being drawn into a pointless discussion.

Before leaving, Kabir gave Rehman a thousand dollars, clarifying that six hundred and fifty dollars was his salary and three hundred and fifty was for his contact in the foreign office.

'Thank you, my contact will be relieved to get the money.' Rehman stopped abruptly, overcome by a fit of coughing. Finally recovering, he continued, 'I was wondering, would it be possible for your boss to make arrangements for my treatment in a good hospital in Calcutta?'

'It's a small favour and I see no reason why he will not help out one of our best assets.' Kabir smiled.

'I am not so sure. I really miss Mr Sohrab. He was always there when I needed him,' Rehman said.

'But if it is just a viral infection, why are you so worried?' Kabir asked.

'I went to see two doctors. Both gave a different prognosis. That is what is bothering me. I will send you all my medical papers in a few days. See what you can do,' Rehman said.

'Of course, no problem,' Kabir responded.

As he stood up to leave, Rehman asked Kabir to lift the mattress of his bed and take the two envelopes lying there. Kabir tucked them into the inside pocket of his jacket before leaving the room. He and his wife thanked Rubeiya for her hospitality and left. His local contact met them on the main road. He told Kabir that no one had followed them at any point of time. Kabir and his wife then got into a rickshaw to head back to their home. They had barely covered two hundred yards when a car swerved dangerously close to the rickshaw. As he leant out to shout at the driver, Kabir saw Jeev at the wheel. The latter asked him to get inside the car immediately. Before the rickshaw puller realized what was happening, Kabir thrust a hundred-taka note into his hand, hustled his wife out of the rickshaw and into the back seat of Jeev's car before quickly jumping into the front passenger seat. He had barely shut the door when Jeev drove off.

'What is Mula doing here?' Jeev asked in surprise.

'Sir, I felt that her presence would provide a good cover story, that we were paying a visit to enquire about a friend's welfare. And if the worst happened, at least she would be able to inform you of what happened at Rehman's place. I thought the NSI might spare her for being a diplomat's wife,' Kabir explained.

'That may be smart thinking, but don't involve her in any future errands. Anyway, what did he have to say about not submitting reports?'

'Sir, his no-show was a false alarm. He is actually very sick. But what brought you to the area at this odd hour?' Kabir asked.

'I had gone to buy some fruit,' Jeev said and smiled. 'Actually, I could sense that you were nervous and you were meeting the source only to ensure that I did not go there and get exposed. That's why I decided to cover you, just in case you were caught and detained by the CEU.'

'Sir, I don't know why Rehman is so unhappy with you. He never tires of comparing you unfavourably with your counterpart in Wellington,' Kabir said, taking advantage of his boss's good mood.

'Go and ask Aroop Das. He will give you the reason,' Jeev quipped.

By the time he dropped Kabir and Mula off and reached home it was 11.40 p.m.

Things appeared to be back on track again. For the next thirteen weeks, the source submitted valuable information that Aroop lost no time in sharing with the government. Rajamohan was so happy that he sanctioned a thousand dollars as an incentive to the source and lauded Jeev for showing rare operational tenacity against all odds. He even called to say that he was looking forward to involving Jeev in far more important projects. Every report that Rehman submitted evoked commendation and the assurance of reward from headquarters. Jeev knew that such comments didn't mean much and were usually made to pacify handling officers, but he was intrigued by Aroop's sudden supportive attitude. When he checked with Barua, he was told that Aroop had gone on a month's leave and in his absence, Barua had been authorized to put up papers directly to Rajamohan.

'So, you are the one who has been manipulating the appreciation of our reports,' Jeev remarked.

'Partly, sir. I highlight the reportable points in the original cable and submit it to Rajamohan. He writes in the margin what is to be shared with the government and what is to be conveyed to you,' Barua explained.

'That's an intelligent way of safeguarding your interests against Aroop's pettiness.'

Kabir, however, was a troubled man. Every time he met Rehman, he felt something was seriously wrong. The source was not his usual self. The duration of their meetings was becoming shorter. He did not want to go to a restaurant, avoided discussions and invariably left in a hurry after delivering cables. He neither explained his odd behaviour nor agreed to suspend working, even temporarily. He did not even talk about Jeev or payments. Kabir had a gut feeling that the relationship was heading for disaster, but when he shared his concerns with Jeev, the latter brushed aside his worries, arguing that Rehman was merely putting up an act to win Kabir over to his side.

'This façade of being an ill-fated man living under the constant scrutiny of both the CEU and myself is merely to extract an extra pound of flesh. It's a pattern that is typical of his behaviour. It's nothing to worry about,' Jeev maintained.

'Sir, I'm not so sure about that. Can I set up a meeting between the two of you? Maybe you will be able to determine why there has been a change in his behaviour,' Kabir suggested.

'Ignore his theatrics. Simply meet him, collect his reports and leave,' Jeev advised.

'Sir, today when I mentioned that he had been rewarded with an incentive of a thousand dollars, he taunted me, asking whether you were paying him to buy his coffin,' Kabir said.

'He finds you friendly and he knows how to use you for his own ends.'

'Sir, he is definitely in some kind of trouble. He looks anxious and edgy all the time and keeps repeating that he is under surveillance and may be apprehended any day.'

'If that is the case, why doesn't he either suspend working for us for some time or end the relationship? Can't you see that his cables continue to flood in week after week and the frequency of reports from his contact in the foreign office has gone up manifold?' Jeev pointed out.

'Sir, maybe he can't help playing with fire. Perhaps he can't do without the money we pay him, and does not want to lose the extra income at any cost,' Kabir argued.

'Fine, then pace out your meetings and stop seeing him for a while. But assure him that he will be paid even if he fails or delays in providing us with cables and reports,' Jeev suggested.

The next meeting, however, took Kabir by complete surprise. Rehman looked cheerful and relaxed. He promptly agreed to go to Lemon Grass for Thai food. He told Kabir that he had spoken to a friend of his who worked for the CEU about his fears. The friend had reassured him that Rehman was not the subject of any of their investigations and had promised to alert him should there be anything in the offing.

'Did his friend ask him why he was suspicious?' Jeev asked when Kabir reported to him on his meeting.

'Rehman told him that he couldn't figure out why the same two persons followed him from the office to his home every evening. His friend explained that the CEU routinely follows employees who work in the top-secret branches of government departments. Since there is an acute shortage of staff, the target of surveillance keeps changing every month. It's possible that the cipher section is currently their target,' Kabir explained.

'So, is he comfortable now?' Jeev asked.

'Yes, sir. I told Rehman that you would be relieved to hear that he had a contact in CEU, since you worry about his safety. I also told him that he would be paid even if he did not submit a report because you did not want to lose him at any cost.'

'What was his reaction?'

'It wasn't charitable. He said he didn't believe that you could either be generous or have concern for other's problems and asked me to tell you that you need not lose sleep over his safety. He once again asked for a hike in his salary but didn't specify the amount.'

'Anything else?' Jeev asked.

'He wants to discuss the foreign office contact with you. He said that Samad was now willing to work as a listed source on a regular salary and that we should run him independently rather than use Rehman as courier.'

'So, Samad is his man in the foreign office. I think I met him some time ago at a reception hosted by the foreign minister. Ask Rehman to set up my meeting with him as early as possible,' Jeev said. 'Has he recovered fully from his illness?'

'Yes, sir. For once he was thankful to you; he said that the medicines you got him from Calcutta were a big help.'

The following week, Kabir tried numerous times to get in touch with Rehman to fix a date for Jeevnathan's meeting, but had no luck. All the source's phone numbers had either been disconnected or deliberately changed. In desperation, Kabir called him at his residence. The operator informed him that all lines in that area were under repair, following the previous night's heavy rains. Next, he went to check the drop boxes, ignoring the mutually agreed upon timings of their clearance. In the drop box behind the Balaka cinema hall, he retrieved a piece of paper on which someone had scribbled:

> *'See me at the Grand Mosque at 7.00 p.m. sharp on Monday. I have something very important to deliver.'*

The writing was not in Rehman's hand.

Kabir showed the note to Jeev, who mulled over its implications.

'Sir, I suspect the CEU has accessed this drop box and left the note for me to pick up. It is possible that the watchers even saw me today when I accessed the box. For all we know, Rehman could have been standing by their side,' Kabir speculated.

'Were you followed at any time during your trip to the drop box?'

'No, sir, I saw nothing unusual.'

'Then why do you suspect that someone may have seen you clearing the drop box?' Jeev asked.

'It's the handwriting that worries me, sir. The CEU may be luring me to the Grand Mosque so that they can apprehend me while receiving classified papers from the source. They may have identified me, but since that will not suffice as conclusive evidence to declare me persona non grata, they are laying a trap to catch me in the act of physically obtaining documents. That will help them seal a case of espionage against Rehman and ensure that I am sent home for being his accomplice.'

'So, what do you think we should do?'

'To avoid falling into this trap, we should ignore this message,' Kabir suggested.

But Jeev thought otherwise. 'I think you should meet him at the mosque. We have to ascertain whether Rehman exposed the drop box during an interrogation or if watchers stumbled on it accidentally,' Jeev said.

'Sir, if I go ahead with the meeting, I will surely be arrested and expelled,' Kabir said, the worry clear in his voice.

'That's a risk you should be willing to take. I will, however, ensure that they do not detain you for more than an hour and that you are assigned to a better station, with virtually no work,' Jeev said with a smile.

'Sir, I have never been afraid for my personal safety, but the situation could be embarrassing for Delhi and for you in particular. The Bangladeshi media and government, and particularly the Nationalist Party and Jamaat, could launch a bitter campaign demanding an apology from Delhi for destabilizing a friendly government and insist on the immediate closure of our unit. Mr Aroop will surely grab this opportunity with both hands and have you withdrawn to headquarters prematurely,' Kabir pointed out.

'Don't worry about that. The important issue now is to find out whether the source has been exposed, which we will only know if you keep the appointment.'

Kabir realized that Jeev would not back down.

'After your first meeting with him, which I remember was at the mosque, have you met him there again?' Jeev enquired.

'Yes, sir, but always on Fridays when it is choked with people. Also, the request to meet in the evening is unusual, as we have never met there at that time,' Kabir said.

'Where in the mosque do you generally meet?'

'We first establish contact on the staircase to the mosque and then move elsewhere, usually to one of the restaurants in the Baitul Mukarram market, or under the covered area to the right of the main entrance gate, or to the adjoining lawn,' Kabir explained.

'So, there is a pattern to your initial meeting.'

'Yes, sir.'

'Going by the drill of your previous meetings, the worst-case scenario would be that Rehman meets you at the stairs and takes you to a rigged restaurant where he hands over classified cables in the presence of waiting CEU officials and the entire proceeding is videographed. Subsequently, you are apprehended and taken away for interrogation. Let us take this as a serious possibility and work out our strategy accordingly,' Jeev said.

'Sir, so you still think I should keep the appointment?'

'Yes, but I will also join you in this mission,' Jeev said.

Kabir was taken aback. He knew his boss's propensity to take needless risks, but he didn't think that he would go this far.

'How long do you generally have to wait before he arrives at the meeting point?' Jeev asked.

'Sir, he always gets there before me. As soon as he sees me approaching the stairs, he makes contact and we quickly leave for wherever it is we decide to conduct the meeting. We then exchange money and cables and discuss anything relevant,' Kabir said.

'Fine. Both of us will go separately to the mosque and wait at different locations till Rehman shows up at the stairs. I will be somewhere in the garden, keeping an eye on the mosque's entrance. You will watch the stairs from the handicraft store near the Bata shop. You will not move unless I ask you to, but keep informing me of his movements over the walkie-talkie. Remember to strictly follow the drill of communicating. In case he walks away and you are unable to contact me, leave immediately without waiting to reach me and follow him discreetly,' Jeev explained.

'Sir.'

'You will not contact Rehman at the stairs under any circumstances. It will be interesting to see how he behaves if he does not find you for more than an hour. We have forty-eight hours before we embark on this trip. Let me know if you have any ideas on refining the plan,' Jeev said.

That night, Jeev told Manini that there was a high probability that he would be expelled from Dhaka and would have to return to Delhi before completing even a quarter of his tenure.

'How soon is this going to happen?' Manini enquired.

'Within the next two weeks.'

'That sounds good. I don't like this place, particularly the unending stream of diplomatic parties. And it will be nice being with our girls again. They will be thrilled to hear the news. I know you will regret losing the foreign allowance, but I am sure you can keep us adequately fed in Delhi with your salary.'

'Will you have no regrets that your husband was thrown out ingloriously?' Jeev asked.

'Not at all. I know you won't be withdrawn by headquarters for financial or moral improbity. If Dhaka finds you too hot to handle, you should be proud of your expulsion. Let me know when I have to start packing,' she said and switched off the light.

Kabir's wife Mula, however, was devastated. She would miss her daily evening visits to the fish market, her group of local friends and her thriving small-scale business of selling Jamdani saris at a good margin in Calcutta, which she sourced directly from the village weavers.

'Why can't you wriggle out of your operational commitment?' she prodded. 'You still have four months left to complete your tenure. Please do something to ensure that we stay here till then. It will help us pay for our son's boarding school fees at R.K. Mission in Calcutta as well as pay off the remaining three instalments for our Salt Lake flat.'

'I cannot let Mr Jeevnathan down. I would never be able to forgive myself if he were to be expelled and I stayed on to complete my tenure. I know he won't relent whether I join him or not,' Kabir said.

Mula fell silent, but she couldn't sleep that night.

As they had planned, Jeev arrived at the venue at 6.30 p.m. and stood at a vantage point from where he had a clear view of the stairs leading to the mosque. Kabir went inside the handicraft shop but had to beat a hasty retreat as it was about to close for the day. He walked a few yards away and took up his position between two kiosks, some ten metres away from the staircase. At 7.10 p.m., Jeev spotted Rehman emerging from the mosque. He went and stood near a lamp post and looked around as if he were expecting someone. Ten minutes later he came halfway down the stairs, stood there for a while and then climbed back up to the main entrance of the mosque. There, he started pacing back and forth until, finally, a man approached him at 7.45 p.m. and handed him an envelope. Rehman opened it, looked at the contents, took out something from his pocket and gave it to the man. After chatting for a while, they came down the stairs together and were quickly swallowed up by the crowd. Jeev looked at his watch. It was 8.10 p.m. He called Kabir on the walkie-talkie.

'I can no longer see them,' Jeev informed him.

'Sir, the source is standing near the bangle shop, but the stranger is nowhere in sight.

'I am listening,' Jeev said.

A couple of minutes later, Kabir updated him. 'Sir, Rehman is sitting on a wooden bench.' Five minutes later came the next update. 'He is now moving towards the entrance of the mosque; he's looking carefully in all directions. I think he's waiting for me, probably to hand over the envelope.'

'Has he ever waited for you for more than ten minutes at a public place in the past?'

'No, sir. Maybe he's waiting it out, thinking that I may be stuck in traffic.'

'Perhaps. But if the envelope is meant for you, why did a stranger hand it over to him in an open place? I suspect he is from the CEU and couldn't hand over the doctored document earlier. What intrigues me most is why Rehman would ask you and the stranger to meet him at the stairs at the same time,' Jeev said.

'Sir, maybe the stranger is Samad.'

'Maybe.' Jeev did not sound convinced. 'Let the source wait,' he instructed.

'Sir.'

'But keep covering him until he leaves. I am no longer in the garden and have left the mosque complex,' Jeev said and disconnected.

After ten minutes, his receiver beeped.

'Sir, Rehman is coming down the stairs, followed by the stranger. They have gone behind the bangle shop,' Kabir reported hurriedly.

'Follow them,' Jeev said.

After a few minutes, Kabir reported that he had lost the source. 'Should I remain in the area to see if he returns?'

'No, I doubt he will. Go home.'

The wait for her husband's arrival had never been so long for Mula. When he finally got home, she burst into tears of relief.

After dinner, as they took their daily stroll in the neighbourhood park, she told him that someone had called in his absence and given a number for him to call back on. Since the number was not familiar, Kabir rang up the following day from the office. It was Rehman who answered the call.

'Why didn't you come last evening?' he enquired.

'I did, but when I saw a man handing over an envelope to you, I got suspicious. This has never happened before. We always meet alone,' Kabir reminded him.

The source laughed loudly. 'Check drop box 4 tomorrow and leave my salary,' he said and disconnected.

The following day when Kabir checked drop box 4, he found an envelope containing nine cables, four reports from the foreign office, a medical prescription and a note.

'The man whom you saw was my contact in the foreign office. I had brought him along to introduce him to you; since your boss is reluctant to meet him, I thought you should meet him instead and assess his worth. You may then be able to persuade your chicken-hearted chief to run him as a regular source. He did not hand over any document but a medical prescription. He wanted your help in getting some medicines from Calcutta. I paid him two hundred dollars yesterday for his inputs. I hope you will reimburse this amount. Will your boss be free to take me out for dinner at Kasturi tomorrow at 9 p.m.?'

Jeev read the note. 'I guess we underestimated his capacity to keep us on edge,' he remarked wryly.

The following day, Kabir tried to contact the source but failed. Later in the evening, he left a note in drop box 4, confirming Jeev's availability for dinner four days later, on Saturday.

A day prior to the dinner, Kabir went to check whether the source had collected the message. The drop box was empty, which meant that Rehman had picked up the note. At 6.00 a.m. on the day they were to meet, Rehman phoned Kabir to let him know that he had reserved a table for five at Kasturi. In addition to Kabir, Jeev and Rehman, there would be a new contact from the home minister's office and a cipher assistant.

'I don't know why he is contacting so many officials on his own,' Jeev said, annoyed, when Kabir briefed him on his conversation. 'He may think that he is helping us in a big way, but he doesn't realize that the more he tries to recruit government employees, the greater is the risk of his exposure. He should first discuss his contacts with me and only if I agree should he set up a meeting. In any case, inviting all of them together is a serious mistake. If he needs more money, I am prepared to give it to him, but there is a professional way of building one's network of agents.'

'Sir, I did question him on the wisdom of inviting his contacts. He assured me that he would not talk of work at the dinner. It was entirely up to us, how we approached them and guided the discussion. But he was certain that you would find them extremely useful and have no reservation in enlisting them as sources. He also said that to avoid his friends suspecting that he was working for the Agency, he would pay the bill, which we could reimburse later,' Kabir said.

'I am still not comfortable with meeting his friends over dinner. If he calls you, ask him to come alone. Also tell him that you will not be there. I want to have a one-to-one meeting to discuss a few sensitive matters,' Jeev advised.

'Sir.'

Later in the day, Jeevnathan cabled Aroop informing him about Rehman's offer to introduce two officials and his reservations about meeting them. He wrote that Rehman had taken on the self-appointed role of talent spotter. The source apparently had no fear of being caught despite knowing that the prevailing surveillance situation was not conducive to even normal source work. He had therefore decided to continue using Rehman as a courier for his contacts, meeting them only later, over a period of time.

Aroop replied within hours that more than the cables that Rehman submitted, it was the reports from his contact in the foreign office that provided insightful and actionable intelligence. The cipher assistant handling China, he opined, would be a better bet than Rehman and he offered to pay any amount to buy his loyalty. In a rare gesture, he approved a reward of five hundred dollars for Rehman for his efforts in locating both officials. He also counselled Jeevnathan not to be overly concerned about the safety of Rehman and wondered why he failed to see the benefits of recruiting the other assets.

'He is a fool,' Jeev muttered as he finished reading Aroop's response. 'I am not going to encourage Rehman to go around bribing officials in sensitive positions to work for the Agency,' he decided.

Kabir was unable to contact Rehman to convey Jeev's insistence on a personal meeting. However, Rehman called at 6.45 that evening. He apologized that the dinner at

Kasturi would have to be called off as he now had to work the night shift as well. He suggested that they could still meet at Haji Biryani at 8.00 p.m. for a quick dinner.

'But my boss wants to brief you on some operational issues. He may not like to come merely for dinner,' Kabir pointed out.

'Okay. Then I can meet him on some other day, but you must come tonight. I will introduce you to my colleague from the cipher section. I haven't told him about our working relationship. You will find him very useful. Quite a few of his colleagues are placed in sensitive positions in various key ministries. If you can recruit him, the Agency will eat out of your hands.'

Kabir agreed and went to clear the plan with Jeev.

Jeev thought Rehman was seriously risking his personal safety and acting in a cavalier fashion. He was also not happy with Kabir for allowing Rehman to speak of operational matters on an open line.

'You should have discouraged him from mentioning the time and place of your meeting and disconnected as soon as he began talking of introducing the cipher assistant,' he reprimanded Kabir.

'I am sorry, sir. But he was speaking from a public booth and had no time to meet me in person.'

'I don't think you should meet him. He has made a habit of cancelling our meetings. He is taking us for a ride. But my greatest worry is that he refuses to take the threat of being watched seriously,' Jeev remarked.

Kabir remained silent.

Jeev sighed. 'Very well. If you still want to take a chance, I will come with you. While you meet the source and his contact at the restaurant, I will keep an eye on the watchers.

But you will enter the restaurant only after Rehman arrives and we have a chance to assess the situation. Keep your walkie-talkie in your jacket. The moment you hear it buzz, leave the area, fast,' he said.

Although Kabir felt that Jeev was making a simple operational meeting far too complicated, he did not protest.

At 7.30 that evening, Kabir parked his car behind the vegetable market near Haji Biryani and took a rickshaw to the restaurant. But he didn't enter, instead positioning himself outside so that he could observe the entrance without being seen. Ten minutes later, Jeev also arrived at the meeting place. He asked the taxi driver to park the car in front of Haji Biryani and waited. At 8.00 p.m., a white Toyota Corolla stopped barely five metres ahead of his taxi. A man emerged from the car and went inside the restaurant. Moments later, Jeev spotted Rehman outside the restaurant, talking to a man in a grey shirt and blue trousers. They chatted briefly and the man gave Rehman what looked like a newspaper from a distance. The man then left and Rehman entered the restaurant. At 8.15 p.m., Kabir called.

'Sir, I saw a man establishing contact with Rehman outside the restaurant. I think he could either be Samad or the cipher assistant.'

'Yes, I saw him too. But I don't think he is the cipher assistant or his contact from the foreign office. You must have seen that the man has already left. He couldn't therefore be the person whom Rehman wanted you to meet. I think he has called you to meet the man who came in the Toyota and is now waiting in the restaurant,' Jeev said.

'Sir, now that Rehman has also gone inside, should I join them for dinner?' Kabir asked.

'You can take a chance. In any case, I am situated close to the entrance of the restaurant. If I see anything suspicious, I will immediately alert you, as we discussed. I wish you the best of luck,' Jeev said and disconnected.

Forty-five minutes later, the man who had arrived in the Toyota Corolla emerged from the restaurant, got into the car and drove off. Rehman came out next and stood outside for a couple of minutes before leaving. Kabir was the last to appear. He quickly spotted Jeev.

'Sir, I have brought some kebab for you,' he said as he got into the taxi. The kebab was in reference to the information provided by Rehman. Jeev kept quiet, firmly discouraging Kabir to say anything further in the taxi. They got dropped off on the main road near the vegetable market where Kabir had parked his car.

'Did anyone else join you and Rehman for dinner?' Jeev enquired after they got into the car.

'Yes, sir. The man who came in the Toyota. He is a serving colonel in Bangladesh Rifles. He was pleasant, and quite talkative. We did not discuss any intelligence matters nor did he show any interest in my background. He spoke mostly about the current impasse in Indo-Bangladesh relations and kept lecturing me on why Bangladeshis dislike Indians. After he left, Rehman told me that he had briefed the colonel about the Agency's requirements and was sure that he would be willing to help us. He claimed that the colonel abhors Pakistanis, Jamaat, ISI and the current army dispensation in Bangladesh. He has strong pro-League leanings and could be a great asset for neutralizing anti-India activities on Bangladeshi soil. Rehman, however, believes that all this will be possible only if you handle him deftly and pay generously.'

'Was he not supposed to introduce his cipher assistant in this meeting? What happened to him?' Jeev enquired.

'Rehman lied to him that the dinner at Haji Biryani had to be cancelled because I had taken ill. Actually, when the colonel confirmed that he would be able to meet, he thought that it was more important for me to meet this officer. The cipher assistant could wait,' Kabir said.

'Did you ask him about the man in the grey shirt and blue trousers who met him outside the restaurant?'

'Yes, sir. He said that he was his brother-in-law.'

'He's lying. I saw them exchange newspapers, which is an unusual thing to do with a brother-in-law in the middle of a market at 8.15 p.m. I suspect he was the cipher assistant who had come to hand over papers to him.'

'Sir, I confronted him with the same doubts. He laughed and showed me the newspaper, which carried a news item with photographs of Rubeiya participating in a function at the school where she teaches. Both came to the market from their respective offices; Rehman to meet me and his brother-in-law to buy vegetables.'

'Did you know that Rubeiya is a schoolteacher?' Jeev asked.

'Yes, sir. She teaches in a private English-medium school.'

'Did Rehman again ask for more money?' Jeev asked.

'Yes, sir. He wants a thousand dollars more every month to keep his contacts productive. He is also keen to meet you to discuss how best to exploit the colonel in case you do not agree to handle him personally,' Kabir said.

'I don't know why he is on a recruiting spree. What if someone betrays him over lower or delayed payments? The greed for money can bring out the worst in even the most virtuous. I will have to tell him to go slow when I meet him, but till that happens, I suggest you avoid meeting him and use only the drop boxes to receive reports and deliver pay packets,' Jeev advised.

By this time they had reached Jeev's residence. Jeev bid Kabir a good night and went in.

Over dinner, Manini told Jeev that their daughter Maitri had called and was excited to hear that they would be returning to India soon, albeit in ignominious circumstances.

'I don't believe that you said that,' Jeev said.

'You are partly right. She was of course very excited, but I didn't use the word ignominious. Anyway, when does our retreat begin?' she asked.

'It looks unlikely now. The police don't want to detain me,' Jeev said, darting her a mischievous glance.

'Who will suffer interrogating such a pompous man? I am sure your reputation of being full of yourself must have reached them by now,' she remarked.

'Isn't it good for me to be arrogant if that will save you from going back to India in shame?' Jeev teased.

Manini merely snorted before going to speak to the cook to finalize the menu for the official dinner they were hosting the following evening.

For once, Aroop Das was happy with Rehman's performance. He credited the source handsomely for not only providing cables with significant intelligence but also for being instrumental in sourcing dozens of high-value reports from his contacts in the foreign and home ministries and recruiting a serving colonel. He could not understand why Jeevnathan was being pig-headed and not seeing the operational opportunities in running those contacts and enlisting them as regular sources. He discussed the matter with Rajamohan, who felt that Jeevnathan was the right man to judge the local security situation and shouldn't be pushed into taking any rash decisions. A week later, Aroop took advantage of Rajamohan's absence from headquarters and discussed the issue with the Chief, in whom he found an ally. The latter felt that caution was the refuge of incompetent officers and told Aroop that he should direct Jeev to meet the new contacts and the colonel immediately. Aroop wasted no time. In a sharply worded cable, he instructed Jeev to not only take over the handling of the three contacts with immediate effect but also to encourage Rehman to rope in as many officials as possible to work for the Agency. He offered to pay any amount for this purpose and sanctioned fifteen hundred dollars as an incentive to the source. In closing, he said that the Chief had reviewed the operation and had found Jeev's caution inexplicable.

'So, he has also rallied the Chief to his side to run the station in accordance with his ridiculous ideas,' Jeev fumed.

However, he neither responded to Aroop's cable nor sought a meeting with the contacts. His years of experience dictated that one didn't allow sources to run the handling officers and plan operations. There was no short cut to painstakingly setting up a network of espionage agents to serve long-term strategic interests.

Kabir followed Jeev's instructions faithfully. He avoided personal meetings but collected reports regularly from the drop boxes. Meanwhile, the colonel started replying to queries that Jeev forwarded to fill in the gaps in information on military matters. Even the cipher assistant had joined Rehman's covert network. Significantly, every envelope that Kabir retrieved from the drop boxes carried a note from Rehman asking for more money to win over more officials and enquiring about the date and time when Jeev would meet the new recruits to get the best out of them. Jeev maintained a studied silence. When pressed hard, Kabir lied that Jeev was occupied with an operation based out of Dhaka, which kept him constantly on the move.

Then one evening, Kabir was surprised to find drop box 3, from which he had gone to pick up material as per the schedule, empty, except for a hastily scribbled note. Rehman sought an urgent meeting exclusively with Jeev to discuss an issue that concerned the safety of both of them. He wrote that he would wait for Jeev two days later in the Bata shop at Baitul Mukarram market at 7.00 p.m. After contact was made, he would take Jeev to a friend's shop so they could talk. If the shop was not acceptable as a meeting place, they could talk while walking behind the row of crowded shops to ensure that their conversation was not tapped by the CEU, he concluded.

'I'll meet him, but tell him that I won't wait for more than ten minutes in the shop,' Jeev said when Kabir told him about the note.

'Sir, may I accompany you?'

'He wants to meet me alone, but I see no harm in your covering me from a distance,' Jeev decided.

Later that day, Kabir dropped a note in drop box 3 confirming that the meeting was on but requesting Rehman to turn up on time. Within hours, the source confirmed on the phone that he would not make Jeev wait.

On the day of the meeting, Jeev left the office early and went home. Over a cup of tea, he told Manini that he would be out that evening as he had to meet someone.

'But Mortaza has invited us for dinner tonight,' she reminded him.

'I'll call him and let him know we'll be late,' Jeev told her before hurrying out of the room to make the call.

She followed him. 'You know that I don't like going late to parties. Why don't you make an excuse and tell him that we won't be able to attend the dinner?' she suggested.

'Mortaza has no problem if we're late and it's only seven now. I should be back within an hour,' Jeev said.

Meanwhile, Kabir reached Baitul Mukarram market thirty minutes early and positioned himself behind a fruit-seller's kiosk. He surveyed the area carefully and soon spotted Rehman. He was standing near an eatery and talking to a man who left after a few minutes. Suddenly, two persons approached Rehman and confronted him. One of them was well built, wearing white trousers and a light-blue shirt and sporting a white skullcap. The other was of medium height and wore a tracksuit and glasses. After a few minutes of animated conversation, both men moved a few yards away and stood near an electrical shop. At 7.00 p.m. sharp, Rehman walked up to the Bata shop and looked around. Five minutes later, he went inside the shop and sat down on a bench. Jeev was nowhere to be seen. At 7.15, Kabir called Jeev in panic.

'Sir, where are you?' he asked anxiously.

'I'll be there in fifteen minutes. I want to give Rehman a taste of how it feels to keep someone waiting.'

'Sir, Rehman has laid a trap. Two men from the CEU are waiting for you. I guess the plan is for Rehman to take you to a predesignated place, where the watchers will subject you to coercive questioning.'

'How can you be so sure?'

'Sir, Rehman first met a man who spoke to him briefly and left. Then came the two watchers who seemed to know him; they too spoke to him before taking up positions near a couple of shops, while Rehman went inside the Bata store to wait for you. One of the CEU watchers has a bag in his hand and is now sitting on a bench in a bangle shop facing the Bata store. Sir, I am sure the bag contains a video recorder, which will be used to shoot your meeting with him. What strengthens my suspicion is that Rehman and this watcher waved to one another.'

'Okay, I will go by your advice. I am going back, but I won't be at home. I have a dinner to attend and I am not sure when I will get home. Call on 28120164 and ask for me in case of an emergency. That is my host's number. Let's discuss our course of action tomorrow,' Jeev said.

'Sir, if you approve, I would like to stay here for a while to observe what they do when they realize that you are not going to show up.'

Jeev weighed the situation before responding. 'Very well, but don't take any unnecessary risks.'

'Sir,' Kabir responded before switching off.

Manini was surprised to see Jeev return early. Jeev told her that he had changed his mind en route; he could not afford to upset his wife, who was a stickler for punctuality.

Rehman, meanwhile, was still inside the Bata shop, clearly on the lookout for Jeev. The crowds were thinning as most of the shops were now closed. At 8.35 p.m., the watcher in the tracksuit went into the Bata shop and emerged shortly after accompanied by Rehman, whom he escorted to where his colleague was waiting. The source appeared to be agitated and Kabir could hear him arguing loudly. Suddenly, the man wearing the skullcap grabbed Rehman by his left wrist and dragged him into the alley behind the Bata store, which was littered with empty shoe boxes. Kabir followed stealthily and, taking cover of the darkness, hid behind a bangle shop. He saw the CEU sleuths shouting at Rehman and shoving him around angrily. All of a sudden, the well-built one stuffed a handkerchief into Rehman's mouth and started punching him. Rehman doubled over and groaned in pain as he was punched and kicked. The beating stopped only when he finally fell to the ground. The man in the tracksuit helped him to his feet, but the tough guy kept swearing at Rehman and pressing his cheeks hard, probably demanding that he provide the details of his espionage network. Kabir tried to overhear what Rehman was saying but could not hear clearly despite moving a few yards closer. What he could make out was that the tough guy was yelling at Rehman and calling him a cheat, traitor and bastard. The other watcher advised him to own up to his mistake. But Rehman kept moaning in pain and shaking his head as if denying the charges. Finally, both toughies conferred with one another, after which the man in the tracksuit spoke to someone on his walkie talkie. They left as soon as he finished.

Rehman remained where he was for some time, leaning against the rear wall of the Bata store. Kabir hurried to a nearby PCO and called the number that Jeev had given him earlier, asking for Jeev. Mortaza, who answered the call, handed the cordless phone to Jeev, saying that Arun wanted to speak to him. Jeev went out to the verandah to take the call. Kabir informed him that the subject was still in the area but had been badly beaten and sought Jeev's permission to stay there until he was sure that the watchers had gone for good and the subject had reached home. He also enquired whether he should provide medical assistance to the subject.

Evidently, Kabir was in a panic.

'Don't lose the kite but avoid running after it,' Jeev cautioned. 'If it flies out of sight, give up the chase and go home. And, under no circumstances will you repair the kite,' he added, keeping his directions as vague and brief as possible in case Mortaza's phone was tapped.

Kabir hurried back to the spot where Rehman had been thrashed minutes ago. He saw the source steadying himself, wiping his face with his shirt and then limping to a public booth. From there, he called someone. After that, he took a rickshaw to the Madhumita cinema hall in Motijheel. It was 9.20 p.m. by then. He entered the alley running along the right side of the theatre. At the far end was drop box 7, into which he stuffed a package the size of a small potato. From there, he dragged himself to a nearby tea stall, washed his face, bought a cup of tea and sank down on an empty bench. Instead of drinking his tea, however, he kept looking down at his feet.

Minutes later, the man wearing the white skullcap appeared again. He had emerged from a car on the main road in front of the cinema and was walking towards Rehman. Unaware of the presence of the man, Rehman abruptly pushed aside his unfinished tea, stood up and started walking away from the toughie, his head lowered, looking at nothing but the road in front of him. Suddenly, he felt someone tapping his shoulder. As he turned to look behind him, the man grabbed his wrist, gagged his mouth with a piece of cloth and dragged him towards the main road where, by now, another CEU man was waiting. They held Rehman firmly between them till a car pulled up and the driver jumped out to open the back door.

But before anyone realized what was happening, Rehman suddenly shoved the man holding his wrist; taken by surprise, the man loosened his grip and Rehman wasted no time in wrenching himself free and sprinting away, taking advantage of the rush of cine-goers emerging from the theatre after the evening show. The watchers quickly got into the car and followed. Kabir saw Rehman weaving his way through pedestrians before he was swallowed by the crowd.

'Sir, I can no longer see Rehman. He has probably been nabbed by the CEU men,' Kabir reported after a few minutes from a PCO.

Jeev was about to disconnect when Kabir exclaimed, 'Sir, I can see him now. He's standing behind Smart video rental, catching his breath. It seems the watchers have missed him.'

'Okay,' Jeev said and hung up.

Barely half an hour later, Kabir called Jeev again.

'Sir, I went and checked the video rental shop. He wasn't there.'

'Okay. Go home. We will discuss this tomorrow,' Jeev said.

'Sir, should I retrieve the packet that he put in drop box 7?'

'Not now, maybe early tomorrow morning,' Jeev advised.

But Kabir was worried. Why would Rehman leave a packet in the drop box after being beaten so badly by the CEU agents? Did it contain something so important that he was willing to sacrifice his life for it? Making a split-second decision, he went to the same tea stall that Rehman had gone to and sat down to have a cup of tea. As he drank it, he looked out for any suspicious activity and when he felt confident that he was not being followed, he went to drop box 7, pulled out the packet that Rehman had stuffed inside and rushed home, taking a parallel route that was more crowded and narrower. He opened the packet only after he reached home. It had a message in Bengali, scribbled hurriedly by Rehman:

> *'The cipher assistant has betrayed me. I spoke to Rubeiya and told her that I may not return home alive.'*

For more than a month there was no news from Rehman. Kabir kept asking Jeev to allow him to contact the source, but Jeev would not agree. 'Let the dust settle. We will eventually have clarity on whether the source exposed our relationship during his interrogation, if his claim of betrayal is true, and whether his offer to meet me at the market was part of a conspiracy jointly hatched by him and the CEU,' he explained to Kabir. Kabir, however, was not convinced about the conspiracy theory.

'Sir, if he was a co-conspirator, why would he allow himself to be beaten up so mercilessly and then leave the note in the drop box, with murderers on his trail? We won't have the answers unless you allow me to meet him and check the drop boxes to see if he has left any messages to explain the circumstances leading to his exposure,' he urged.

'Forget Rehman. I have no sympathy for him. He is responsible for what has happened to him. I think you need to learn to approach your sources like a nurse or a landlord. No undue attachments and no hard feelings when your patient or tenant leaves. Sources come and go in an operator's life. You must develop the ability to remain unaffected if and when they disappear,' Jeev counselled him.

Kabir thought his boss sounded like a mercenary but said nothing, feeling helpless.

'Come to think of it,' Jeev continued, 'Rehman was his own nemesis. He paid the price for his overconfidence. In any case, he has given us enough. You can't expect such relationships to last forever.'

Nothing, meanwhile, appeared in the vernacular or English newspapers about the arrest of a Bangladeshi national for espionage. Jeev casually asked his legal contacts if they had heard of any such case, but no one could confirm the filing of charges in the courts against any individual for leaking information to foreign agencies. With no breakthrough in sight, Jeev wrote to Aroop, apprising him of the loss of Rehman. However, it was Rajamohan who cabled after a week. He wrote that it was a huge setback and felt that Jeev had been right in opposing the source's running amok with his initiatives. He hoped that Jeev, being the officer on the ground, would know best how to extricate the Agency from this potentially embarrassing situation.

Arun was, nevertheless, still perturbed. He wished Jeevnathan had made some effort to bail the source out. Over the past few months, he and his wife had come to like Rehman and Rubeiya a lot for their hospitality and warmth. They had regularly exchanged gifts and delicacies on festive occasions, keeping Jeev in the dark. No wonder Arun felt wretched for not being able to do anything for his friend. For nights he couldn't sleep properly, troubled by vague dreams of Rehman groaning in pain in the interrogation centre and of Rubeiya crying and yelling at him for forcing her to sell their household possessions to survive.

Driven by remorse, Kabir finally decided to defy his boss and check the drop boxes. He began with the one that was right behind an air-conditioning repair shop near his house but which had rarely been used by the source because of its proximity to his house. To his surprise, he found more than a dozen scribbled notes, a few of them ineligible, and an envelope, all covered in dust. He collected them hurriedly and ran back to his house. He placed them on the dining table before carefully opening and reading each one. They were all from Rubeiya. It was obvious she had used that particular drop box because she had wanted Kabir to access her letters easily. Each note was a plea for financial help, but the last one, which was in the envelope, betrayed her extreme desperation. She had taken the grave risk of writing in her own hand and signing her real name. It was heart-wrenching:

> *'I don't know if you have been receiving my letters. In case you haven't, let me inform you that Nayeem has been arrested. He tried to escape to your country and was in hiding for a few weeks but was eventually caught. They have been interrogating him for over a month. I have not been allowed to see him. I desperately need some monetary help. But please do not visit my house. My cousin Anees, who is a lawyer, knows about the case and has met my husband three or four times. My brother Bashir also keeps meeting him. He tells me that Nayeem looks drained and is unable to speak coherently. Why have you turned your*

back on someone who put his life at stake for you? Why are you so cold and indifferent? Is this how you repay your friends?'

-Rubeiya'

'So, Nayeem is his real name. He is neither Rehman nor Shiraz,' Jeev mused as he finished reading the note. 'For once, I cannot be angry with you for your foolhardiness. It's good that you disobeyed me and checked the drop box.'

'Sir, we must provide financial assistance to Rubeiya immediately. It would be inhuman to abandon her and her children in their darkest hours,' Kabir pleaded.

'None of these notes seem to have been written recently. Maybe she gave up on us and approached others for financial help,' Jeev said.

'Sir, even if she did, can't we give her something to meet her legal expenses? If you agree, I can discreetly meet her cousin to find out how much he would need and how far we have been exposed,' Kabir suggested.

'This operation is over. You are no longer Kabir. It's time for you to return to your real self and name. I cannot pay his wife when her husband is no longer working for us,' Jeev said.

Arun was astounded by the insensitivity of his boss.

They never discussed the case thereafter.

The Aftermath

Jeev was busy reading a report when his assistant buzzed him. 'Sir, there's a man on the line who insists on speaking to you but refuses to give his name. He is also not willing to explain the purpose of his call.'

'Put him through,' Jeev said.

'Hello, it's me. I had an envelope delivered to your residence. You will find it flattering,' the caller said.

'Thank you. But for you, the man would not have survived. It's a debt I will never be able to repay,' Jeev said.

'Don't worry, we will settle it over a cup of tea,' the caller assured him before disconnecting.

When Jeev reached home that evening, the guard handed him an envelope. It was stapled and sealed with tape on all sides. Although he was curious, he kept it in the drawer of his bedside table to read later as he had to leave soon to attend an official dinner. After he returned, he wasted little time in taking out the envelope from the drawer. As he switched on his bedside lamp, Manini pulled the bed sheet over her head and turned away from him so she could sleep. Jeev pulled out a single sheet of paper from the envelope. On it was a typed, unsigned message.

'Thank you for the help. Typically, your delivery mechanism left no footprints. Except for Rubeiya, neither my friends nor relatives nor my lawyer could identify the source that provided the funds to fight my case and save my family from starvation. I have lost my job but I am a free man now. The case fell through in the absence of any evidence. I never had any admiration for you while we lived dangerously together. But I was wrong.'

Jeevnathan felt a lump in his throat and stared at the roof.

'What is it that you are reading? If you are finished, please switch off the light,' Manini said.

'Read it,' Jeev said and gave it to her.

She switched on her bedside lamp and read through it.

'I always knew that you were a good man but a bad husband,' she remarked, patting his cheek lovingly.

The Zero-Cost Mission

Amar Bhushan joined the Indian Police Service in 1967 and was assigned to Madhya Pradesh. For seven years, he dealt with crime and law and order problems but remained a reluctant policeman. When the opportunity for working in intelligence organizations came, he grabbed it and never looked back till he retired as the chief of India's foremost technical intelligence agency. He began the second innings of his career by briefly serving in the BSF intelligence, State Special Branch and Intelligence Bureau and ended up with working in the Research and Analysis Wing for the next twenty-four years.

His last published work, *Escape to Nowhere*, remained on bestseller lists for eleven weeks. He lives with his wife and daughter in Bangalore but seldom misses an opportunity to visit his granddaughters in the US and his mother in Jasidih, a village in Jharkhand.

The Zero-Cost Mission

Amar Bhushan

HarperCollins *Publishers* India

First published in India by
HarperCollins *Publishers* in 2018

Building 10, Tower A, 4th Floor, DLF Cyber City, Phase II,
Gurugram Haryana – 122002, India
www.harpercollins.co.in

2 4 6 8 10 9 7 5 3 1

P-ISBN: 978-93-5277-903-1
E-ISBN: 978-93-5277-904-8

Typeset in 10.7/13.6 Cardo at
Manipal Digital Systems, Manipal

Printed and bound at
MicroPrints India, New Delhi

To my wife, Manju, whose bittersweet remarks kept me on course to survive and prosper in jobs that offered huge temptations to stray easily from principles and professional integrity.

Preface

Within days of the release of my book *Escape to Nowhere* in 2012, a junior colleague who had served under me years ago came to see me. He marvelled at my good fortune to survive in India's external intelligence service, an agency that thrived on cronyism, mediocrity and arrogance. He recalled how he had been made to suffer for his operational wizardry and for his habit of speaking his mind. He wished that he had been more tactful and had not followed my example of fighting those who created obstacles in serving the country's security interests. Before leaving, he wondered whether I could share his travails with readers, as I had shared mine in my book. I asked him to write about his operational experiences and send them to me.

In the following days, he spoke to other colleagues who had similar experiences. Within weeks, I was flooded with accounts of operations run by junior and mid-level officers, filling hundreds of pages. While sifting through the material, I couldn't help but admire their courage and their ability to suffer and survive. I sat down to write, to acknowledge their heroic actions and to explain how they operated despite the indifference from petty and incompetent officers and hostile working conditions, both in India and abroad.

I have avoided mentioning too many technical details to make the narrative intelligible. Despite pruning the material, the narration is not always fast-paced because life in intelligence agencies is often dull and repetitive. For operational security, I have opted for the medium of fictionalized storytelling so that sources are not exposed and their trust is not betrayed. The plot of each operation, however, stays close to the facts. Most of the characters have since died. Those who are still around will hopefully enjoy revisiting the part they played in carrying out the missions. But some who hindered missions may find reason to be less than pleased.

Of the thirty-nine operations that I received material on, I have selected two for this book as part of the Spymaster Series. Each one is different in terms of the nature of the assignment, the method of execution, the characteristics of the agents employed and the eccentricities of the handling officers. Hopefully, the officers who led the operations and their agents in the field will have reason to cheer when they see their accomplishments in print. It is my hope that their experiences will help intelligence officers understand that there is no greater joy than executing missions. To readers who are not familiar with the workings of the Agency, these stories will help unravel the mystery behind running agents, provide an insight into the trauma an agent goes through while undertaking perilous operations and highlight the qualities that make a real spymaster.

The Zero-Cost Mission

Delhi, 1992–93

It was 7.30 p.m. Jagjit Singh Aulakh, chief of India's external intelligence agency, left the South Block of the Central Secretariat, which housed the Prime Minister's Office and the Ministry of Defence, after attending a meeting chaired by the principal secretary to the prime minister. As he walked to his car, he called the officer on special duty (OSD) to find out if Vijay Shukla, the desk officer for Bangladesh operations, was still waiting for him. The OSD confirmed that Shukla was indeed still in the office. For a moment, Aulakh thought of asking Vijay to go home but changed his mind in view of Vijay's repeated insistence on the need to reach a quick decision regarding his plan for a top secret operation. Always correct in his manners, he called Vijay, apologized for keeping him waiting, and informed him that he was on his way to the office.

As the car glided down Rajpath, Aulakh reflected on the pointless deliberations he had just witnessed. Attended by the cabinet secretary, the secretary (personnel), the principal secretary to the prime minister and himself, the meeting had lasted for over two hours and ended with the stalemate intact. They had continued to drag their feet over breaking

the eight-month-long impasse over filling two posts for special secretaries from a panel of four eligible officers to manage critical operational responsibilities. Aulakh found the indecision and the repetition of the same arguments frustrating; no one was willing to do what was necessary to break the logjam and accommodate the Agency's two most deserving officers. The problem lay in the fact that these officers did not have the minimum of eight outstanding reports during the last ten years to back their promotion. One of them, whom he wished to promote out of turn, could not be considered because he was junior by a whisker. On the other hand, the officers in the running who had both seniority and excellent records were poor analysts and failed operatives, and did not deserve to hold crucial positions at such a senior level. It was disheartening to see the mandarins eventually decide to keep all appointments on hold till retirements settled the issue in due course. He was apprehensive about how his officers would take the decision and how it would impact their motivation to continue to work with the same verve and commitment.

For the first time in his long career, Aulakh regretted his habit of recording generous comments in the annual confidential roll of officers irrespective of their level of competence, thus enabling them to vie for promotions for the wrong reasons. However, when it came to assigning work, he seldom compromised on merit. He had a keen eye for picking the right officer for the right job. This knack enabled him to handle officers of all calibres, from below average to outstanding, with ease. He would often say that an army with only outstanding generals was a recipe for disaster; it would breed jealousy, indiscipline and fierce rivalry, eluding consensus on any plan or initiative.

As the driver turned into the lane leading to the entrance gate of the Agency's headquarters, Aulakh saw that apart from the executive floor, where his office was located, and the seventh floor, which housed the offices of Vijay and his boss Vishwanath Reddy, the building was almost entirely dark. Everyone had left, barring those who manned the twenty-four-hour operational services. The driver stopped the car briefly at the gate for an electronic verification and then drove past the sprawling lawn towards the main building, which was bathed in muted light. The area around was enveloped in total darkness and nothing was visible beyond five metres. This was for security reasons.

As soon as Aulakh entered his office, he buzzed the OSD and asked him to send in Vijay. As he waited, he pulled out a file marked 'Top Secret' from a drawer in his desk. As he was perusing its contents, Vijay entered, greeted the Chief and sat down.

'Have you discussed this proposal with Reddy?' Aulakh asked after he finished reading the proposal.

'Yes, sir. He has made no changes,' Vijay said.

'He should be involved in our discussion. Let me see if he is still around.' Aulakh dialled Reddy's extension and when he answered, requested him to join them.

Reddy thought of informing the Chief that he had to leave soon as it was his fifty-eighth birthday and his wife and children were planning to take him out for dinner, but he decided against it, thinking it would be better to first find out why the Chief wished to speak to him at this hour.

As he walked down the stairs to the Chief's office, he called his wife to let her know that he had been delayed and would join them at the restaurant as soon as he could.

Vishwanath Reddy, head of the South Asia division, was an intelligence officer by default. Given a choice, he would have loved to be an officer in the Foreign Service, or a banker, or an event manager. His heart lay in handling administrative matters, pursuing welfare schemes for employees at the Agency, and socializing and interacting with politicians, businessmen and well-placed bureaucrats. He was extremely good at making friends, not necessarily for intelligence purposes. The secrecy that inevitably shrouded an intelligence officer's life weighed on him, as he loved to live an open and extravagant life. He enjoyed seeking and doling out favours, generously entertained friends and colleagues, and took pride in his connections with power brokers from diverse fields. He was sharp-witted, intelligent and charming. No one had ever seen him angry or ruffled.

Reading reports received from sources in the field and analysing developments were, however, anathema to Reddy. So he spent the better part of his career serving outside the Agency's claustrophobic working environment. When he had to finally return to the Agency after a long stint at the Ministry of External Affairs as the chief liaison officer, Aulakh surprisingly assigned him to handle the volatile South Asia region. Initially he was lost, his experience being in handling administration and protocol, but slowly, aided by common sense, astuteness and a team of bright and dedicated officers, he began running his area of responsibility well. Shrewd as he was, he gave his officers full liberty to operate and they, in turn, rewarded his faith by executing operations successfully, leaving no room for the Chief to complain or be disappointed with his performance. In due course, Reddy rose to become the Chief's right-hand man.

When he entered the office, he saw the Chief going through a file and Vijay Shukla seated before him, waiting patiently for him to finish. The Chief waved him to a seat.

'I've gone through Vijay's proposal. But as you are the head of the Southeast Asia division, I want to hear your view on the operation's feasibility before making my final decision.'

Reddy realized that the Chief was referring to Vijay's proposal to destroy the facilities of the Jamaat-e-Islami of Bangladesh along the Indo-Bangladesh border. Ever since India's partition in 1947, Jamaat had been promoting Pakistan's political, strategic and religious interests in the then East Pakistan. During the 1971 Bangladesh Liberation War, it actively collaborated with the government of Pakistan and the Pakistani Army, and fiercely fought the Bangladeshi nationalists who were demanding a separate state due to the years of suppression of their cultural and linguistic identity and exploitation of their economic resources. Following the creation of Bangladesh in 1971 with the help of the Indian Army and the formation of a government by the liberationists in Dhaka, Jamaat went into hiding temporarily, but it slowly emerged as a powerful Islamist group committed to setting up an Islamic state in Bangladesh ruled by the Sharia legal system. Unable to reconcile itself to the liberal values of the new political dispensation dominated by the Awami League, Jamaat emerged as Pakistan's frontline arm in the east of India to contain Indian influence in Bangladesh, neutralize the consolidation of liberal forces in the country and help in the growth of political parties, social and religious groups that opposed India. As such, it lost no opportunity to carry out anti-India activities. Its camps and facilities were being

used to help Pakistan's Inter-Services Intelligence (ISI) send its agents to carry out acts of terror in India and to push illegal Bangladeshi Muslims into the country to alter the demography of the eastern border states of Tripura, Assam, Bihar and West Bengal.

'Frankly, I'm not convinced we can pull it off,' the Chief remarked as he returned the file to Vijay. 'You make a strong case for hurting Jamaat and the urgent need to carry out an operation against them, but the plan of action you have outlined is complicated. I agree with your assessment that we have to stem the influx of illegal Bangladeshi immigrants, but the means you have suggested to accomplish this seem unrealistic. For example, the amount of service money you have requested for this mission is very high. It will be difficult for me to allocate it from my existing resources. And if I approach the prime minister for additional funds, he may not approve of the proposal. In fact, he is likely to reprimand me for encouraging officers like you to entertain wild, irresponsible and dangerous ideas and may even question my intent regarding the timing of the operation, given that state assembly elections are scheduled to take place in three of the eastern states during the next eight months. We all know the crucial role illegal Muslim immigrants play in swinging the electoral fortunes in West Bengal, Bihar and Assam.'

'Sir, if the problem is of funds, we can scale down the size of the operation and tailor it to fit our budget,' Vijay submitted.

'If you do that, your purpose will not be fully served. I'm not in favour of a piecemeal approach,' the Chief countered.

'Sir, our first strike can be smaller in magnitude; it can serve as a dress rehearsal, and if it succeeds, we can follow it

up with more strikes at regular intervals, denying Jamaat the opportunity to regroup,' Vijay argued.

'No dress rehearsal. In a year's time none of us will be here, handling our current responsibilities. It is anybody's guess whether our successors will choose to continue with this operation.' The Chief paused and gazed out of the window thoughtfully before continuing. 'Honestly, I am not convinced that the destruction of a few Jamaat facilities will significantly disrupt the infiltration of militants and illegal immigrants into India. Corrupt security forces and immigration officers, touts and smugglers, and conniving inhabitants on either side of the border will continue to facilitate their entry,' the Chief pointed out.

'Sir, my purpose is to at least start somewhere. The hope is that the execution of this plan will send a strong message to collaborators and force them to fall in line.'

'Perhaps, but how do we convince the prime minister that this operation will benefit India's long-term security interests?'

'Sir, is it necessary to involve the prime minister at this stage?' Vijay asked. 'I doubt any prime minister would like to be direct party to a project of this nature, whatever the justification. But as intelligence officers, we cannot remain mute witnesses to the steady invasion of India by illegal immigrants, criminals and terrorists from Bangladesh, aided and actively abetted by Jamaat and the Harkat-ul-Jihad al-Islami.'

'How certain are you about this invasion?' the Chief probed.

'Sir, the statistics are provided in the report's annexe. Between 1950 and 1995, infiltration increased by 650 per cent, the number of madrasas along the border increased

from twenty-eight to over 1100, and the number of districts in the four bordering Indian states where Bangladeshi Muslims have upset the electoral equation has jumped from two to twenty-one. At this rate, by 2050 the demography of the eastern states will have changed completely. It is just a matter of time before we begin to hear whispers followed by a clamour for a referendum by the migrants to seek a separate nation for themselves along our eastern border,' Vijay pointed out.

'The situation cannot be so bad,' the Chief interrupted. 'Are these facts and apprehensions based on briefings from your paid sources?'

'Largely, but I have also checked the census figures, the internal assessment reports of the Ministry of Home Affairs and field enquiries conducted by several NGOs. Most of these reports have been deliberately suppressed for reasons of political expediency. But the most significant information was provided by a source in the Bangladesh government's Ministry of Agriculture. According to him, in early 1992, the United Nations World Food Programme seriously considered reducing its quota of food for Bangladesh following field enquiries conducted by the Population Fund, which showed a significant drop in population in all border districts of Bangladesh. Apparently, the inhabitants had crossed over to India and during the same period, the number of immigrants on our side was reported to have gone up substantially. Is this not sufficient indication of the frightening direction in which we are headed?'

'And what direction would that be?'

'Sir, we are staring at a second partition of India and I don't know if we can afford to procrastinate further on this

issue. It is only a matter of time before someone rallies them to attain this goal,' Vijay asserted.

Reddy thought Aulakh deserved credit for allowing Vijay to argue his case so strongly. No other chief of the Agency would have tolerated Vijay, an officer three ranks his junior, to argue so forcefully for his views and openly contradict him. The Agency had a history of arrogant chiefs who wielded fear as a weapon. There were, of course, a few gentleman chiefs, but Jagjit Singh Aulakh was clearly a cut above all of them.

'I understand your concerns,' the Chief finally conceded, 'but let's not forget that destroying the Jamaat camps and their religious institutions can lead to swift and bloody consequences. It may result in a violent backlash against Hindus in Bangladesh and later, reprisals against illegal Muslim immigrants in India by angry Hindus. Besides, Indian political parties that have vested interests in encouraging the illegal immigration will surely cry foul and accuse us of acting like Rambos against hapless Bangladeshis coming to India in search of bread and butter for their survival.'

'Sir, if you believe that there is some merit in my proposal, let me give it a shot,' Vijay urged. 'We may not be able to tear down the Jamaat infrastructure completely, but I am confident we can force them to think twice about sending their agent provocateurs and volunteers to India.'

'Vijay, my biggest worry is the method you propose to employ in dismantling their network. You are planning to use your existing sources, many of whom must be under the surveillance of the Bangladesh Special Branch. You will be asking these sources to hire volunteers who have not been tried and tested by you in any operation. Then, you want to

use these same volunteers to procure explosives from local defence depots which are heavily guarded. This will not only put their lives at risk but will also require superhuman effort to hide our complicity. If the Bangladeshi intelligence agencies or our political leadership smell our involvement, I will find it very difficult to either deny or justify our unilateral action.'

'Sir, I am absolutely certain of covering our tracks,' Vijay claimed, and drew the Chief's attention to the measures he had proposed for ensuring the secrecy of the operation.

At this point, Reddy looked at his watch surreptitiously. It was half-past nine. He imagined his wife and children must have reached the restaurant and placed their orders. Impatient to leave, he decided to prompt the Chief and Vijay to conclude their discussion, which he thought had already become more of an academic debate. 'Sir, I have discussed this proposal threadbare with Vijay and I think it is workable,' he said.

'I still believe it will not be appropriate to launch such a major offensive without informing the prime minister. He may not agree, he may dispute our facts and find flaws in our arguments, but he should not be kept in the dark about a mission that involves entering a sovereign country to carry out a violent offensive against a political party that is part of the government in power,' the Chief opined.

'Actually, sir, I feel we should keep the PM out of it,' Reddy suggested. 'If we inform him of the proposal, he will have to take a position. If he says no to the operation, he may regret his helplessness to take a call when it is needed most. And if he agrees, he exposes himself as communal before a nation that is perennially caught in the crossfire between secularists and pragmatists.'

'Fine, if both of you insist on executing the operation, please amend the proposal so as to give absolute deniability to the PM and to the Agency. I want clarity on how you will shield him from the accusation of interfering in the internal politics of Bangladesh. As it is, the ruling Nationalist Party is always looking for an excuse to whip up anti-India sentiment in Bangladesh. If it finds out that the Agency has orchestrated attacks against Jamaat, which is after all its alliance partner in the government, it will raise hell, to the glee of their friends, Pakistan and China,' the Chief cautioned.

'Sir—'

'I also want details on how you plan to handle the retributive response of the League in case Jamaat attacks them for collaborating with the Agency. You must ensure that the Nationalist Party does not lend its resources to Jamaat for taking their retaliation deep inside India.'

'Sir, one option is that we send feelers to the League before launching the operation and warn them to be prepared for a backlash from Jamaat. The other is that we let events dictate the nature of the response of the League, Jamaat and the Nationalist Party following the destruction of the staging camps,' Vijay said.

'I don't think the League will want to be sucked into our fight against the Jamaat,' the Chief averred. 'Especially since it is struggling to stay politically relevant—it is being steamrolled in the parliament on all issues, its leadership and cadre are under constant physical attack and the morale of its workers is in total disarray. I doubt it will be willing to divert its focus from taking on the Nationalist Party to fighting Jamaat on our behalf,' the Chief argued.

'Sir, when it comes to Jamaat, the League will do anything. It has not forgotten the mass murder of thousands

of Bangladeshi freedom fighters and intellectuals by Jamaat mercenaries at the behest of the Pakistan Army during the Liberation War of 1971. Unlike the Nationalist Party and its allies, it has not forgotten our contribution to their freedom struggle and to the reconstruction of their ravaged economic, political, educational and administrative institutions. They would be more than willing to join us in this mission,' Vijay pointed out.

'I don't agree,' Reddy interrupted. 'We must avoid prior consultation with any party or individual for an operation of this sensitivity.'

'Agreed. But let's say I clear the proposal. Are you sure Atul Kulkarni, who is currently in charge of the Calcutta office, is the man to carry it out?' the Chief enquired. 'He is not cut out to handle operations that require precise and detailed planning and complete control over their execution. He also suffers from a misplaced notion of his operational abilities and comes up with impractical ideas. My fear is that he will alter your plan with his own misguided ideas, making a mess of its execution.'

'Vijay has some ideas on this,' Reddy said. 'He suggests transferring Atul to headquarters and bringing Sujal in from Hyderabad to take over in his place.'

'But Atul has not completed even a year in the Calcutta office. He is bound to protest his premature withdrawal to headquarters and will insist on knowing why he is being transferred so soon,' the Chief said.

'Sir, in that case, perhaps we can allow Atul to continue in Calcutta and assign Sujal as his deputy with the understanding that Sujal will run this operation on our behalf and report only to us,' Vijay said.

'Wasn't Sujal posted to Hyderabad only five months ago?' the Chief asked. 'I don't want to uproot his family again. I suggest you look for another officer.'

Reddy glanced at his watch. It was 9.45 p.m. Before Vijay could say anything, he requested the Chief to allow him to leave.

'Yes, of course, I think we're done here for tonight,' the Chief agreed. 'Vijay, I want you to submit a list of officers from whom we will choose the one who is best suited for this mission. And please amend the plan of action, giving total deniability to the PM and the Agency. We can finalize the officer who will be in charge of the operation after I come back from tour. 'Reddy, if you can wait for five more minutes, we can leave together.'

'Actually, sir, my wife and children are waiting for me in a restaurant. Today is my birthday,' Reddy, who had run out of patience, finally announced.

'Oh! Many happy returns of the day! I'm sorry for detaining you; why didn't you tell me earlier?' the Chief asked.

He shook Reddy's hand warmly, hugged him and requested Reddy to let him speak to his wife. Reddy dutifully called her; the Chief apologized to her for delaying Reddy and promised to make amends by taking them out for dinner.

Reddy left soon after that and arrived at the restaurant as his wife and children were about to finish their dinner. As usual, they refrained from enquiring about the reason for his delay and instead ordered his favourite whisky, followed by food. They were used to him missing such family festivities.

When they finally got home, they found a large bouquet of roses waiting for them. It was from Aulakh.

Vijay Shukla, however, had stayed back at the office at the Chief's request. After Reddy left, the Chief asked Vijay if he had any particular reason for trusting Sujal to undertake the operation.

'Sir, once you put him in charge of any operation, you can rest assured it will be carried out flawlessly,' Vijay replied. 'He is aggressive, motivated and possesses the courage of the devil. He accesses his targets directly, neutralizes the worst of his foes in no time, has no qualms in using and dumping sources and enjoys experimenting with unorthodox methods to execute his task. Sir, he has only two drawbacks. He is prone to overpaying his sources and is averse to keeping his seniors updated on the progress made in an ongoing operation and any difficulties that he runs into before it is finally over.'

'I don't know much about him. But several senior officers have complained to me that he is opinionated and highly critical of those who do not favour him. I believe he also has a tendency to flout instructions and ignore departmental guidelines,' the Chief said, a frown creasing his brow.

'Sir, that may be true, but he is a rarity among field operatives,' Vijay clarified. 'He worked with me for a few years and I saw him functioning from close quarters. He has a real talent for planting sources in what appear to be inaccessible targets. What separates him from most of us is his love for accomplishing the impossible. I am sure that when I brief him, he will jump at the offer. He won't hesitate to take up the challenge, in spite of the inconvenience the move to Calcutta will cause to his wife and children.'

'He must be really good, given the passion with which you are advocating his case,' the Chief remarked. 'I may just take a chance with your project and this officer. But before I transfer him to Calcutta, I want you to speak to him and gauge his reaction to the offer. Also, keep Reddy informed of our final decision. You can schedule our next meeting two weeks from now. Invite Sujal as well.'

Aulakh concluded the meeting.

Vijay collected the file and left. He was happy that he had succeeded in getting the Chief on board for a project that had become his obsession ever since he had joined the Bangladesh desk.

The next day, Vijay updated Reddy on his discussion with the Chief and on his plan to sound out his friend on his likely transfer to Calcutta.

'Are you sure he will accept the offer?' Reddy asked.

'I know Sujal. He likes his ego to be massaged, so I plan to tell him that he has been specially picked to undertake an operation in Bangladesh on behalf of the Chief,' Vijay confided. 'Besides, the operation will also provide him with the opportunity to renew his contacts with his old friends and assets in Dhaka.'

'Sounds like you plan to make an offer he will find hard to refuse,' Reddy said, smiling.

'Yes, although the only possible hitch is his wife's poor health. He may refuse to move because of it.'

'Let's speak to him. But we should tell him to come to Delhi—I'm not comfortable mentioning anything about such a sensitive project on the phone. You can brief him on the proposal in my presence, and we can get his views on its feasibility as well as his reaction to relocating to Calcutta.

I see no point in sending an unhappy man to run such a difficult mission.'

'I agree, although I can't think of anyone better than Sujal to head this operation. In fact, I had only him in mind to run it when I first conceived the plan.'

'Then let's hope he agrees,' Reddy concluded.

Sujal was intrigued to receive a cryptic cable from Vishwanath Reddy, who wanted him to take the first available flight to Delhi. The cable gave no indication of why he was being summoned. He had never worked under Reddy nor had he ever had anything to do with Southeast Asia, the latter's regional responsibility. Staying true to his obsessive sense of discreetness, he called no one at headquarters to find out more about the possible agenda for the meeting. He took the flight to Delhi the following morning and headed straight to the Agency headquarters. He rang up Reddy to announce his arrival from the reception desk. Reddy, who was busy in meetings, asked him to come to his office. He gave Sujal a folder and suggested that he go through its contents carefully and return to discuss them that evening at five.

His curiosity more than piqued, Sujal retired to the library and began reading through the document. He quickly realized that the subject matter of the note did not relate to the Middle Eastern countries that he was currently handling but rather to Bangladesh, which he had handled several years ago. It was a thirty-two-page top-secret operational plan, accompanied by several annexes and maps, but without any mention of who had authored it.

He glanced through the portions that sought to justify the objective, smiled as he read the plan of action and put several question marks in places where the logistic requirements were listed out. He spent most of his time in going through the concluding paragraphs in which firewalls to protect the Agency from exposure were suggested. After that, he noted down the points that created doubts in his mind and needed clarification. But he still could not understand why Reddy wished to take him into confidence regarding a project that sought to destroy Jamaat's facilities inside Bangladesh. He guessed that Vijay might have advised Reddy to seek his input on the plan's feasibility because of his past experience in handling Jamaat during his tenure in Dhaka. But that was years ago, Sujal pondered. He had of course remained abreast of developments in Bangladesh since then but only through the newspapers and friends occasionally visiting from Dhaka. Knowing it would be pointless for him to speculate further on why he had been summoned, he decided to wait till he met with Reddy to get some answers.

At 5.00 p.m. on the dot, Sujal entered Reddy's office for the meeting. To his pleasant surprise, Vijay was already there. They exchanged smiles. He quickly realized that Vijay was very much a part of the proposed plan and had probably drafted it.

'Were you able to finish reading Vijay's magnum opus?' Reddy enquired, confirming Sujal's suspicions regarding the author of the plan.

'Yes, sir. I read the operations part thoroughly in which Vijay lays out the proposed steps to achieve the objective and explains how he is going to secure the footprints of the Agency,' Sujal replied.

'Is it possible to execute this operation?' Reddy asked pointedly.

'Theoretically, yes. A lot, however, will depend on who will supervise its execution, the kind of sources that will be deployed on the ground and whether headquarters will fund it without raising an eyebrow,' Sujal said.

'Vijay is of the view that only you can pull it off. His plan is to relocate you to Calcutta and entrust this operation to you,' Reddy said.

'He is an old friend, and his faith in me is flattering, but I have been in Hyderabad for only six months. My kids have just started a new term in school. My wife underwent a major surgery last month and is making a slow recovery,' Sujal hedged.

'I know the relocation will be hard on you. I will certainly bring your concerns to the Chief's notice, but if he insists on handing over the operation only to you, I'm afraid you will have to move,' Reddy said.

After a moment's pause, Sujal asked, 'Sir, why this urgency to attack the Jamaat posts?'

Reddy looked to Vijay to respond.

'The fact of the matter is that we can no longer defer action. Any more dithering will make our security situation extremely vulnerable,' Vijay stressed.

'I see,' Sujal mused, almost to himself.

'How much time will you need to wrap things up in Hyderabad and move to Calcutta?' Reddy enquired. 'We will of course meet all your relocation expenses,' he added.

'A fortnight, sir. I can bring my wife and children later, after finding suitable accommodation and a good school for the kids,' Sujal said. 'However, I must have blanket approval

to travel between Calcutta and Hyderabad whenever my wife needs me till such time as she moves.'

For Reddy, it was strange to see a junior officer dictating terms without squirming. He, however, agreed to Sujal's condition.

'Sir, there is one more thing. I know Atul Kulkarni is currently heading the Calcutta office. But it will be difficult for me to work under him. I had the misfortune of serving under him for a year. I don't want to revisit his pettiness, his shallow operational ideas, his nagging questioning over expenses and his vengeful attitude. In fact, I will spend more time in managing him than in working on the project. Why don't you leave me out of it and let him run this operation under your direct supervision?' Sujal asked.

'We have already considered that option and rejected it. We cannot entrust such a sensitive responsibility to someone who has impractical ideas, can neither win nor run a source and who invariably annoys assets and loses them. Atul is good at planning grandiose operations but cannot execute them. He will simply ruin it. There is no room for anyone to make the slightest error of judgement in this plan,' Vijay averred.

'If he cannot be trusted to run such an operation, why don't you transfer him elsewhere?' Sujal suggested.

Realizing that the conversation was going nowhere, Reddy intervened. 'Sujal, the Chief has already approved your posting to Calcutta.'

'So I don't have a choice,' said Sujal.

'No, you don't,' Reddy responded with a smile. 'But I am going to inform Atul that in addition to functioning as his deputy, you will be handling an operation independently

under my direct supervision and you are not to be questioned about either the disbursement of funds or any travel undertaken by you to bordering areas or to headquarters in this connection.'

'Sir, he is not the kind to accept this arrangement willingly. He may not protest officially or express his unhappiness openly, but he will try to ruin my career by providing negative feedback in my annual confidential reports. He has always been a silent assassin for those who refuse to be bulldozed by him,' Sujal pointed out.

'Don't worry. I will take care of that,' Reddy assured him.

'Sir, I have one more request. Please send the service money for this operation separately to me by name,' Sujal urged.

'That's a minor issue. You have ten days to read through the proposal thoroughly and clarify any doubts with Vijay. The Chief would like to discuss the plan with all of us before taking a final decision. Your transfer order, although approved on file, will be issued only if he clears the operation. Vijay will let you know the date and time of our meeting with the Chief. I imagine he will have several questions to ask you regarding the viability of the plan, how it will be executed in the field and by whom, and how you plan to disburse service money. Come prepared for a grilling,' Reddy warned.

'Sir, the only thing I need to know is the objective, which has been clearly outlined in the note. But I will only be able to work out the operating details after I select suitable volunteers for the job, identify the targets and obtain from my agents an accurate estimate of ground difficulties. The plan may have to undergo several mid-course corrections to make it effective. I am also not in a position at the moment to give an estimate of the amount of service money that will

be needed. For that, I have to first talk to my field operatives to assess the degree of risk that each one will be exposed to during the plan's execution. Sir, if you have entrusted this operation to me, allow me to handle it the way I see fit,' Sujal requested.

Reddy was impressed by Sujal's audacity and clarity of mind. For a change, he was interacting with an officer who was sure of himself, held his ground firmly and had no qualms about questioning directives if he felt they would compromise a mission. He realized that he would be dealing with an officer who was not only demanding, but was also challenging to handle.

'What if your plans fall short and you fail?' Reddy asked.

'Sir, that is a chance that you will have to take with me,' Sujal replied calmly.

'I have no quarrel on that score. Let's see what the Chief has to say about your suggestions,' Reddy said. He shook hands with Sujal, saying that he hoped to see him soon.

After they left Reddy's office, Sujal reproached Vijay for sucking him into a complicated operation.

'But wouldn't you like to get involved in such an operation?' Vijay probed.

'I would, but only if a Jeevnathan is there to stand by me. I don't have a clue about Reddy's leadership qualities or style, nor do I have an idea of the stuff that the Chief is made of. Since there are more chances of failing in such operations, my fear is that they might dump me halfway through and later accuse me of wasting crores and embarrassing them,' Sujal opined.

'Neither of them will let you down,' Vijay assured him. 'Reddy may not be able to guide you in conducting the day-to-day operations, but he will back you till the end.

The Chief is also extremely supportive and encourages differing points of view,' he confided.

Somewhat reassured, Sujal bid Vijay farewell and left for the airport to catch the evening flight to Hyderabad.

Later that night, Sujal shared what had transpired in Delhi with Arpita, his wife. He had been agonizing over whether it would be right for him to subject her to a relocation given her fragile health. He knew he had to warn her of the possibility and take into consideration her reaction before he took a final decision on Reddy's offer.

'You always think of your work,' Arpita was quick to react.

'I understand your feelings and I did express my reservations regarding undertaking this assignment, but Reddy wouldn't listen,' Sujal said.

'I don't grudge you, your passion for conducting intelligence operations. You know that I have always supported you in your work. I even sacrificed my dream of establishing myself as an accomplished Odissi dancer and accompanied you to Dhaka to serve as a housewife,' she said.

Sujal kept quiet, fondly holding her hand.

'I never complained about that,' she continued. 'I thought it was my destiny. But think at least of our children's future. If we keep moving, their education will suffer.'

Sujal listened, mostly in sympathy.

'I have yet to recover fully from my surgery, but that doesn't seem to bother you. I know you will still go because you love your job more than anything else,' she accused mildly.

'That's not true,' Sujal interrupted.

'If you have to move to Calcutta, I suggest you make arrangements to send us to Cuttack to live with my mother. With my brother's help, I will try to get the children enrolled in a public school there,' she stopped speaking, feeling tired.

'You have been a great support in whatever little I have achieved in life,' Sujal said fondly. 'Unlike other officers in the Agency, I have discussed almost every source and operation with you because I deeply value your opinion as well as criticism. There is no question of my accepting this operation if it means that you will have to go to Cuttack and manage without me.'

'I know you are a very loving husband. But look at my health. It is better that I spend some time with my mother to recuperate. Besides, I will feel terrible if you refuse the Chief's offer because of me. You have always enjoyed taking up challenges and in this case the Chief has specially selected you to undertake an operation,' she tried to reason half-heartedly.

'I won't get involved in anything that requires me to leave you to fend for yourself. The Chief can make a negative remark in my annual confidential report for refusing, but I am prepared for that. As it is, my record is littered with indifferent remarks. So one more won't make any difference to my career,' Sujal said.

'I would like you to run operations that make you happy, but I am also worried about our safety. Do you remember how relieved I was when we finally left Dhaka at the end of your tenure? The General had threatened to kill all of us if you did not stop mobilizing the opposition against him. Fortunately, he did not carry out his threat. This time

you are taking on Jamaat, which is deadlier, more brutal and determined to hit back. It doesn't matter if we are in Calcutta or elsewhere. They will find us through their network of contacts and target us,' Arpita said.

'I told you I will not go to Calcutta and if Reddy insists, I will go on extended leave. Now, relax and go to sleep,' Sujal reassured her.

Over the next few days Arpita reflected on their discussion. While she was concerned about the impact the move would have on the children's education, and genuinely worried about the danger the operation could expose the entire family to, she also knew that Sujal was excited by the opportunity. He thrived on running such operations. She knew what she had to do.

'I know your heart lies in taking up this operation,' she told Sujal over breakfast a few days later. 'You must not get swayed either by my health issues or by my concerns regarding our safety,' she insisted as Sujal tried to interrupt her. 'Please call Vijay and tell him that you will accept the assignment. You can leave as soon as possible. I will stay back in Hyderabad for a couple of months. Once you find a house and a good school for the children, we will join you there. Besides, Calcutta is not very far from here and you can always rush back if there is an emergency.'

'I can't leave you behind to take care of yourself and deal with any post-operative problems. More than ever, you need my help now,' he said, pouring coffee into her mug.

'Don't rush into a decision you may regret later. You have never worked under this Chief. Who knows, this

operation may give you an opportunity to show him your worth as an operative, and bring a turnaround in your career,' she argued.

'I no longer care about my career. Besides, I hear that he is timid, tries to please everyone, from the brightest to the most useless, and is averse to violent operations. I doubt if Reddy has even discussed this proposal with him. Aulakh is currently on tour and is scheduled to return next week. I am to go to Delhi to discuss the feasibility of the operation with him when he's back in the office. For all you know, he may scrap the project after I highlight the risks involved in undertaking it,' he opined.

'Then let's wait and hear what he has to say before taking any decision,' Arpita counselled.

Sujal's meeting with the Chief turned out to be brief but positive. Reddy, Vijay and his combative colleague from Hyderabad met the Chief in the mini-operations room adjoining the Chief's office. As soon as they were all seated around the oval table, the Chief got down to business.

'Reddy, have Vijay and you briefed Sujal on the plan?' he enquired.

'Yes, sir. He agrees with the concept but not with our suggestions on how to execute it. He insists on conducting it on his own terms, which he will spell out in due course after you clear the proposal in principle,' Reddy said.

'May I know what your terms and conditions are?' the Chief asked, looking at Sujal.

'Sir, I ask for three assurances. First, no one will waver and scrap the operation or curtail once it has commenced.

Second, if you foresee any difficulties in making available the required resources, I should be informed before the start of the operation. And lastly, if I fail to deliver, I shall not be subjected to any departmental scrutiny.'

'Are you suggesting that none of us will have any role in this except for making the required resources available to you?'

'Yes, sir.' There was complete silence for a few seconds.

'That's an audacious self-belief. Nevertheless, I am willing to take a chance on you and this operation for Vijay's sake. He has enormous confidence in your operational ability,' the Chief said. 'You can go ahead, but do not misuse my blanket authority to ride roughshod over your colleagues or execute the plan recklessly. You will report only to Reddy, should you need any assistance. I need not stress how important it is for you to remain extremely discreet for the duration of this operation. In fact, it's probably best if you are less visible at headquarters.'

Sujal found it strange that the Chief was approving the operation not because of any compelling reason to act against Jamaat but because of his fondness for Vijay.

'Sir, can I say something on the feasibility of this operation?' Sujal asked after some hesitation.

'You can discuss that later with Reddy and Vijay. If you have the slightest doubt about its workability at any stage, just walk out of it,' the Chief advised.

'Sir, I am reasonably confident of pulling it off. The only thing that concerns me is Atul's reaction when he sees me sidestep him repeatedly. He has a history of ruining operations out of jealousy,' Sujal pointed out.

The Chief felt awkward listening to a junior officer speaking ill of his senior and hence chose not to respond

to the insinuation. Instead, he enquired about his wife's health.

'She is better now, but it may take a few more months for her to recover fully,' Sujal said.

'Give her my regards,' the Chief said and thanked Vijay and Sujal, signalling that they could leave. However, he requested Reddy to stay back.

'I don't know if Vijay has made the right choice in assigning the operation to this officer,' the Chief confided. 'I find him presumptuous and arrogant.'

'I don't know much about him, but Vijay swears by his ability. He showed me the files of a few operations in which Sujal was involved. It is remarkable how he handled them singlehandedly. What struck me is his ability to adapt and improvise his modus operandi in a changing situation and his capacity to remain unfazed in the midst of reverses,' Reddy said.

'Did he tell you which aspects of the plan he disagrees with and why?'

'No, but he has promised to come back with his comments on Vijay's proposal by tomorrow evening.'

'How much service money does he expect us to provide?'

'He refused to hazard a guess, but on my insistence, he said that it could be in the range of rupees 5 to 7 crore,' Reddy said.

'What is he talking about? Is he going to bomb the whole of Bangladesh that he needs so much money? He may be an excellent operator but don't concede to everything that he asks for. Also, keep a close watch over his handling of service money and make sure he doesn't defy any rules of business while running the operation,' the Chief advised.

'From the little that I know of him, I don't think he will embarrass us,' Reddy said. 'My sense is that he will go boldly after the target as long as he has our backing. He often credits Jeevnathan for shaping him into what he is today. I think he expects us to take a cue from his mentor who, he says, trusts his officers blindly and provides service money without asking any questions.'

'Now I know where he gets this streak of talking defiantly and dictating terms,' the Chief remarked.

Reddy left as the OSD entered the room to inform the Chief that his next meeting was about to start.

After their meeting with the Chief, Sujal reflected on the latter's reactions as he sat waiting for Vijay to finish with work before they headed out for lunch. He thought Aulakh was decisive and appreciated his openness in listening to a junior officer's opinions and concerns. But he also felt that he was overly concerned with the fear of exposure and its chain reaction, which meant that he might pull out if the operation ever ran into problems. For a moment, he toyed with the idea of raising his estimation of the logistical requirements to such an extent that Reddy would find it impossible to meet them, thus forcing him to either scrap the mission or replace him. But that would be mean, he knew. Moreover, it would rob him of the opportunity to re-establish contact with his old friends in Dhaka. A thought suddenly occurred to him. Vijay had told him that the Chief was worried about the fallout from the violence the operation could entail. So why not try something different to achieve the objective without spilling a drop of blood? Struck by a bizarre idea, he

reached for the phone and dialled a number. A lady finally answered after it rang for a while.

'Am I talking to Mrs Hossain?' Sujal enquired.

'Yes, but who are you?' she asked.

'Rehena, this is Sujal Rath. Do you remember me?'

'Of course, Sujal-da. What a surprise to hear from you after such a long time! Where have you been hiding all these years? I tried your number several times but you never answered. Even our common friends in Delhi were of no help in tracing you,' Rehena chattered on, true to her excitable nature.

'I will explain everything when we meet. I am in a bit of a soup right now. Can I talk to Shariful?'

'He has gone to Sylhet but should be back soon. Why don't you give me your number? I will ask him to call you back as soon as he returns. Are you speaking from Delhi?'

'I am travelling in Europe. Please tell him that I will contact him tomorrow morning at seven, Dhaka time,' Sujal said.

'I will make sure that he is available to receive your call. How is Arpita boudi doing?'

'She is fine. I have a surprise for you,' Sujal said, but the call was abruptly disconnected before he could continue. He tried calling back but gave up after a few failed attempts.

'Who is Shariful?' enquired Vijay who had overheard the conversation.

'He is a Jamaat ideologue and more of a friend than a source. He teaches physics at Dhaka University. He may be of some help in your operation,' Sujal said.

'Why did you lie to his wife about travelling in Europe? She can easily call your bluff by tracing the number.'

'I have my reasons,' Sujal responded cryptically.

'Why do you need to talk to a Jamaat leader for an operation that aims to destroy Jamaat facilities?'

'I will explain everything in due course, but let me first talk to him,' Sujal replied.

'You shouldn't have used the office phone to call your contact. It compromises our security.'

'You have to take your chances with me,' Sujal said.

Early the following morning, Sujal called Shariful Hossain, a senior and respected leader of Jamaat-e-Islami of Bangladesh. He was a strange fit in his party. Though deeply religious, he was not a fundamentalist and was the main architect behind bringing Jamaat into the mainstream of political activities. Never shy of opposing Jamaat's disruptive agenda in his typically suave and erudite manner, he was both resented and admired by the party leadership. Sujal had got to know him when he was posted in Dhaka, hitting it off with him from the day they met at a party hosted by a playwright, known for his plays that caricatured religious bigotry as well as unbridled permissiveness. In due course, they not only became good family friends but also met frequently to discuss political developments. Sujal had never revealed his intelligence background to Shariful and Shariful had never probed, perhaps assuming that there was more to his job as a diplomat than met the eye.

'It's very nice to hear from you,' Shariful responded warmly after Sujal announced himself on the phone. 'Rehena told me that you had something urgent to talk about.'

'I need to speak to Crescent on a matter of mutual interest. Can you please set up a meeting with him?'

Crescent, a rabid fundamentalist and the prime conspirator behind the mass killing of liberal and secular Bangladeshis during the Liberation War and an architect of the close working relationship between the Nationalist Party and Pakistan, was the de facto head of Jamaat. He had built his organization around an intense hatred for India and the establishment of the rule of Sharia in Bangladesh.

'What should I tell him is the purpose of your meeting?' Shariful enquired.

'I can't discuss that on the phone, but it is very important,' Sujal said.

'Let me see what I can do. You know how distrustful he has been of even genuine overtures from Indian officials and Indian intelligence agencies. But I will definitely try to persuade him,' Shariful assured Sujal.

'Tell him he has nothing to worry about. After all, I will be meeting him in Dhaka, in his den, unescorted, so if anyone has to be chary, it is me and not him,' Sujal pointed out.

'Give me your number,' Shariful said.

'If possible, please speak to him today to gauge his reaction. It's better if I contact you. I will call you back at 1.30 p.m. your time—' The line got disconnected. Sujal tried a few times to call Shariful back but finally gave up.

With nothing to do but wait, Sujal went back to sleep. He woke up late in the morning, had a leisurely breakfast and sat down to read through Vijay's proposal once again and note down his questions and comments. Shortly after noon, he walked to Khan Market nearby and called Shariful from a public booth.

'I'm sorry to call you before the decided time. Given the network problems, I didn't expect the call to go through on my very first attempt,' Sujal began anxiously.

'Your timing is perfect,' Shariful assured him. 'I have just returned after meeting Crescent. It went well—he readily agreed to see you and didn't seem too interested in knowing the reason behind your visit. In fact, I was a little surprised at his eagerness to meet you. But you will have to be in Dhaka within a couple of days. He is leaving for Saudi Arabia early next week and may not return for two months.'

'Let me see how quickly I can arrange my travel documents,' Sujal responded and thanked Shariful profusely.

'Bring Arpita along if it is possible. Rehena will be happy to see her and share with her all the gossip about Dhaka's liberated wives and girlfriends,' Hossain said.

'She would have loved to meet Rehena but she is not yet fit to travel. I'll bring her along the next time for sure,' Sujal promised.

'Is she not well?'

'She recently underwent surgery,' Sujal said.

'Oh! I'm sorry to hear that. I hope it's nothing serious.'

'She is feeling much better and should be back on her feet in a couple of months,' Sujal assured him and thanked him again before hanging up.

Vijay was horrified when Sujal told him of his plan to travel to Dhaka and asked him to arrange for his passport, visa and tickets under a cover name.

'Why on earth do you want to meet Crescent clandestinely when the plan is to wipe out his facilities and kill his volunteers?' he asked.

'Like the Chief, I want to avoid bloodshed. You may find this strange coming from someone who believes in executing missions ruthlessly, but it's never too late in one's life to approach operations differently. Crescent owes me for a variety of reasons. So I thought why not take a chance and persuade him to withdraw his staging posts, stop pushing Bangladeshis illegally and sending militants, and close down camps where terrorists are being groomed by Jamaat and the ISI,' Sujal explained.

'You really are crazy.' Vijay shook his head. 'We want you to mount a violent offensive and here you are, talking like a peacenik. Do you realize that your meeting will not only ruin the element of surprise in the operation but also give Crescent a reason to accuse us later of attacking their facilities inside Bangladesh?'

'I am aware of these possibilities but see no harm in warning him of serious consequences if he refuses to fall in line,' Sujal maintained.

'I have nothing against your trip to Dhaka to meet your old friends, but I have grave doubts about whether anything will come of your meeting with Crescent,' Vijay said.

'I cultivated and groomed him assiduously, more as a friend, during my Dhaka days. My effort was to blunt Jamaat's hostility against us and use him to wean his outfit away from the vice-like grip of the ISI. He seemed to have begun to appreciate our political and strategic concerns in the region, but before he could bring about a substantive change in his outfit's policy towards India, my assignment in Dhaka ended. I didn't keep headquarters in the loop regarding my efforts with Crescent because your predecessor was dead against the very idea of engaging with Jamaat leaders at any level.'

'How can you even entertain such wild ideas that defy ground realities? Do you really believe that these murderers can ever be reformed?'

'Tell me, am I solely responsible for this operation or not?'

'You are.'

'Then let me run it my way. I am sure you were aware of my operational eccentricities before suggesting my name to Reddy.'

Vijay laughed at that. 'You're right. But I don't have the authority to approve your visit to Dhaka. We will have to speak to Reddy about it.'

Sujal agreed and they headed to Reddy's office.

The latter fully endorsed Vijay's concerns but finally ruled in favour of Sujal.

'I am also convinced that the visit will not serve any purpose, but since we have put our faith in you, Sujal, we must give you a chance to do things your way,' Reddy decided.

'Sir, I think we should inform the Chief. Anything can happen, given who Sujal will be meeting,' Vijay suggested.

'If you want to scuttle my trip, please go ahead,' Sujal interrupted. 'But I see no point in involving the Chief in every small matter. From what I know of Crescent, it is unlikely that he will agree to my proposal. Nonetheless, I think it's worth taking a chance, especially if it will avoid bloodshed and a costly operation. And please don't be worried about my safety. In case I don't survive the trip, simply inform Arpita. She is braver than you think.'

Vishwanath Reddy pondered for a while, admiring Sujal's courage of conviction. Hesitant to agree in spite of

Sujal's arguments and assurances, he asked Sujal whether he would like to rethink his plan before Vijay arranged for his tickets and travel documents.

'Sir, the risk that I'm taking is small. Vijay can tell you how many times I tempted fate in the past and came away without a scratch,' he said.

'Fine. You can go ahead and plan your visit. Vijay will arrange for your documents and the funds to cover your travel expenses,' Reddy finally agreed. 'Incidentally, have you had the time to write down your thoughts on how you plan to approach the operation?'

'Sir, that discussion will have to wait till I return from Dhaka. Everything depends on how Crescent reacts to my proposal,' Sujal responded.

Reddy nodded and wished him luck. Sujal left, followed by Vijay.

As they walked back to his office, Vijay asked, 'Have you told Arpita about your proposed move to Calcutta?'

'Yes, we did discuss the pros and cons of the move. Initially, she was against the idea of uprooting the family again. I agreed with her; I can't expect her and the children to suffer an unsettled life for the sake of my career. Besides, she needs me now more than ever to take care of her health. I told her that I wouldn't accept the offer. In fact, I almost sent you a cable declining the assignment, but she changed her mind and insisted that I accept the challenge. I was adamant, but she wouldn't let me refuse the offer. We finally agreed that we would all move to Calcutta.'

'She really is a unique woman.' Vijay smiled. 'Did you tell her that I was the villain who plotted this conspiracy and that she should curse me and not you? I feel guilty for sucking you into this operation, but I also know that

you alone can pull it off with any chance of success,' he said.

'I also accepted because I know this operation has been your pet for years. Anyway, let me know as soon as my travel documents are ready.' Sujal paused as he spotted the Deputy Chief approaching them. He greeted Sujal warmly and asked him to join him later for a cup of tea. Sujal told him that he had a flight to catch for Hyderabad that evening, but promised to call on him when he visited headquarters next.

'How is it that you know the Deputy Chief so well?' Vijay enquired.

'He is one of the few officers who values my work. The others are Jeevnathan and Vijay Shukla,' Sujal said with a smile.

By now both had reached Vijay's office. Sujal collected his briefcase, bid Vijay farewell and left. In the lift, he was joined briefly by Atul Kulkarni. They exchanged perfunctory nods before Atul got off on the fourth floor. Sujal guessed that Reddy must have summoned Atul to inform him about his posting and to instruct him not to meddle in the project. He hoped Atul would take his cue from Reddy and would allow him to run the operation on his own terms.

Vijay kept his word and dispatched Sujal's travel documents the next day. But subsequent events did not auger well for the visit. On the day of his departure, Arpita complained of acute abdominal pain and fever. Worried, Sujal called the doctor and decided to cancel the trip, but Arpita insisted that he go as planned and made the doctor assure him

that there was no need to panic. Then, a few hours before leaving, Sujal tried to contact Shariful, but no one answered the phone. Once again, he contemplated postponing the visit as he wanted to be sure that Shariful was in Dhaka, but eventually he decided to take a chance.

He landed in Calcutta, from where he was to take a connecting flight to Dhaka. But then came another twist. While he was waiting in the lounge for the flight to Dhaka to be announced, the head of the Agency's unit at the Indian High Commission in Dhaka entered the lounge. Sujal had no option but to greet him. He soon realized that they were both booked on the same flight to Dhaka. To maintain the secrecy of his visit, he lied to the Agency officer, telling him that he was on his way to Delhi. Then, to avoid any further questions, he excused himself saying that his flight was boarding. From the lounge, he quickly went to the Biman airline counter and bought a ticket for a flight to Dhaka that was scheduled to depart two hours later. However, the flight was delayed by hours due to bad weather in Dhaka. When it finally took off at 3.00 a.m., it was pouring and the aircraft had to circle over Dhaka airport for close to an hour before it eventually made a rough landing.

Sujal's problems did not end there. As he was walking towards customs, he made brief eye contact with an immigration officer whom he knew; Mizan had been of great help during his previous assignment in Bangladesh. Sujal quickly ducked out of sight and waited as Mizan craned his neck in all directions to locate him. Once he saw that Mizan had given up on finding him and was moving away, he went through customs, hopped into a taxi and headed to his

hotel. By the time he checked into Hotel Sonargaon on Kazi Nazrul Islam Avenue under a cover name, it was 8.00 a.m.

After a quick wash, he called Shariful, but a maid answered the phone. She informed him that the Hossains were out of town but were expected back soon. An hour later, he called again. This time, finally, Rehena answered.

'Shariful has been anxiously waiting for your call since day before yesterday,' she said and asked for Sujal's number and the name of the hotel where he was staying.

'I did try to reach him a few times yesterday, but no one answered,' Sujal said.

'We had to suddenly leave for Khulna to attend his grandmother's funeral and returned an hour ago because we expected that you would try to contact us,' Rehena told him.

'Please ask him to call me as soon as possible. I'm staying at the Sonargaon Hotel, room number 204,' Sujal said.

'I hope you know that you are dining with us tonight. I am planning to invite a few of our common friends. They would love to see you and catch up with you after so many years.'

Sujal thanked her and hung up. He didn't like the idea of the dinner as it would expose him to too many people. But before he could figure out how to handle the situation tactfully, Shariful called him. He told him that the 'event' had been scheduled for 8.00 p.m. in his house. Discreet as ever, he said nothing further and disconnected.

Feeling relieved for the first time since he had left Hyderabad, Sujal had lunch in his room and spent the rest of the afternoon catching up on some much-needed sleep. He woke up at 6.00 p.m., refreshed. An hour later, he took

a taxi to the Hossains' house on Road No 10A, behind Kalp Neer, arriving five minutes early.

Shariful received him warmly and took him to his study, where Crescent was already waiting for him. Upon seeing him, he quickly stood up and stepped forward to grasp Sujal's hands.

'Brother, I cannot tell you how happy I am to see you back in Dhaka after seven long years. I thought I would never see you again till Hossain came to tell me that you wanted to meet,' he said.

'I am glad you agreed to see me at such short notice,' Sujal responded, smiling.

'Where have you been all these years?' Crescent enquired.

'I was serving abroad, but I always kept abreast of events around you. I heard that you have been getting politically stronger in partnership with the Nationalists in the government. After I returned to India earlier this year, I was told that under your leadership, Jamaat had seen a phenomenal growth in the strength of its cadre and has emerged as a formidable force in most college and university campuses. When I spoke to Shariful bhai, he wasn't sure if you would be able to find the time to see me, given your preoccupation with party work and impending visit to Saudi Arabia. And yet you agreed to meet,' Sujal said.

'This is the least I can do for a friend,' Crescent remarked.

'I gather your party has also made huge inroads into the electoral base of the League.'

'We are trying. We faced very rough times due to the League's belligerent attitude. Knowing of your proximity to the League's leadership, I often thought of contacting you so that you could advise them not to push us too hard. But I didn't have your number,' Crescent said.

By now both had moved to a sofa and settled down. Shariful offered to serve refreshments but both declined simultaneously.

'I shall leave you both to continue your meeting as I know Sujal has come here specially to discuss something with you in private,' Shariful said as he turned to leave the room.

'No, no, Shariful bhai, please join us. I would value your perspective and opinion on the issue that brings me here,' Sujal said, insisting that he stayed.

'Very well, anything to help an old friend.' Shariful smiled as he sat down.

'What is it that you want to discuss?' Crescent asked.

'We have reports that Jamaat has considerably stepped up hostile activities along the Indo-Bangladesh border and is using its units and madrasas to send Pak-trained terrorists and Bangladeshis illegally into India. I have brought you an offer in this regard. We will address all your legitimate concerns, including those regarding the ban on travel to India, and allow your leaders and volunteers to visit India for lawful purposes. In return, you will abandon your confrontationist posturing and cease all hostile activities along the border,' Sujal said without beating about the bush.

'You have obviously been misinformed by your sources. These allegations are totally baseless,' Crescent countered. 'It is true that we have augmented our presence along the border, but this is purely for benign political and religious purposes. Our long-term goal, as you know, is to marginalize those who are still hounding us in the name of protecting the ideals of liberation and are converting the younger generation into enemies of Islam.'

'If you continue to toe your old line of regressive and radical Islamic politics and continue to fight the League, I doubt your party can ever be politically rehabilitated in this country,' Sujal opined. 'Political arrangements are never permanent. Today you have the Nationalists on your side. Tomorrow, the League could form the government and invite you to govern in a coalition. But if you continue treating them as the enemy, you may be squeezed dry if they come to power, which is not very unlikely.'

'That's precisely why we want to expand our electoral base and add teeth to it so that when needed, we can bite and effectively blunt the League's assault, with or without the Nationalists,' Crescent said.

'But why do you want to get sucked into this vicious cycle of suspicion, hatred and clashes against each other? This country is already an Islamic Republic and no government can reverse this reality. For you, it is only a question of accepting the bitter truth that Bangladesh is now liberated from Pakistan and you are the sons of this soil, which you should nurture in a spirit of accommodation rather than enmity.'

Crescent remained quiet, appearing to reflect on Sujal's words. 'I am sure you didn't come here to lecture me on deserting the Nationalists to join your pro-liberation friends,' he remarked eventually.

'You are right. I have been deputed by my prime minister to obtain an assurance from you that Jamaat will not permit its volunteers and facilities to be used for carrying out subversive activities in India either on its own or on behalf of the ISI.' Sujal deliberately positioned the proposal as coming from the prime minister to lend it greater weight. 'Since you once called me a brother, I volunteered to come

here and take this opportunity to persuade you to cool your intense animosity towards India and the League. Especially as doing so will be in your long-term interest. But if you insist on pursuing your radical Islamic agenda by creating trouble for us and eliminating your rival countrymen, who knows what the consequences may be.'

'Why do you repeatedly bring Pakistan and ISI into our discussion?' Crescent asked. 'The only link that we have is with Jamaat-e-Islami of Pakistan. There is absolutely no quid pro quo with ISI with respect to any of their operations directed against India,' he emphasized.

'But our reports suggest otherwise,' Sujal countered. 'They reveal that your cadres have been regularly dumping explosives and arms in several hideouts along the border, providing shelter to illegal emigrants at your forward posts and allowing the ISI to use your madrasas and units as launching pads to push terrorists into India. If you want, I can share some of the audio and video evidence we have gathered of the instructions that your leaders have issued to your bordering units and madrasas on how and when to send these terrorists and emigrants across.'

'There is no such thing happening. I am sure your Agency has fabricated this so-called evidence,' Crescent retorted.

'Please understand my situation. I have reason to believe that if you do not stop your unfriendly acts, Delhi may take action. Since you are more than a friend to me, I thought of warning you before it is too late to take any corrective measures,' Sujal explained.

'What action is your government contemplating? Are you planning to kill our volunteers and bomb our

headquarters and facilities by sending fighter aircrafts?' Crescent said sharply.

'I don't know. Maybe I'm reading too much into the signals from Delhi. But I see no reason why you should be working to destabilize India unless you are under compulsion to do so at Pakistan's bidding,' Sujal argued.

Crescent remained silent for several seconds. 'Let me return from Saudi Arabia. Then you can show me the evidence of our alleged complicity,' he finally said. 'Jamaat is a purely religious organization and we are involved in politics only to safeguard our religious interests and not to threaten India's security,' he reiterated.

Shariful looked at Sujal in some discomfort.

'But what you are saying does not make any sense to Delhi. The government questions why you are financing the dailies *Inquilab* and *Sangram*, which regularly pour venom against India. What interest do you have in inciting your cadre against our government and its treatment of our Muslims? Do you think that Indian Muslims need the crutches of Jamaat-e-Islami of Bangladesh to survive and prosper? Delhi's perception is that you are preparing your volunteers to fight, kill and die for your vision of an Islamic state not only in Bangladesh but also in India. My fear is that if you continue along this path, you will permanently alienate a powerful neighbour and moreover, will become a pariah in your own country,' Sujal cautioned. Although he was brutal in his choice of words, he spoke softly, without aggression.

'I don't agree. It is my duty to keep our workers informed of the atrocities committed against our Muslim brothers in India and agitate the conscience of Islamic countries by highlighting those incidents,' Crescent said.

'Your party seems determined to dig its own grave. Despite all your claims and rhetoric, Indian Muslims are not going to migrate either to Bangladesh or to Pakistan. You are creating enemies for nothing,' Sujal said.

'And what is your formula for Jamaat? To become friends with a Hindu India?' Crescent asked.

'First, we don't live in a Hindu India but in India. Second, if you promise to abandon your siege mentality and stop pursuing hostile activities against India, I will actively help you to be a part of the liberal democratic forces in Bangladesh, which in the long run may well serve as your insurance against the war cries of the League and its supporters for your head,' Sujal explained.

'And if I don't promise, will you join forces with the League to clean us up?'

'Why don't you look at your situation realistically? The Indian political leadership treats you as untouchables and a large section of Bangladeshis look upon you as enemies of the nation. If you give up your politics of hatred and enmity, I can persuade both Delhi and the League to accept you as partners in running the country together.'

'I don't think you will ever forsake your friends in the League or help us financially and politically,' Crescent insisted. 'Ultimately, it is our physical strength that will see us through troubled times and enable us to capture power and establish the rule of Sharia in this country.'

'That is unlikely to happen in Bangladesh. It is a predominantly liberal and democratic society and has a history of fighting to protect and preserve its political and cultural identity. I doubt if you will be able to Talibanize the Bangladeshis' belief.'

'It is not easy for me to comment on your proposal. I don't think either the Chairman or the cadres will accept your arguments. It is going to be extremely difficult for me to persuade them to accept that a Hindu India can be their friend and that they do not need an armed cadre to ensure their survival,' Crescent said.

'You can discuss the matter within your party. My offer is on the table, but don't delay in taking a final decision,' Sujal warned him subtly.

'Why do I get the feeling that you came here only to threaten me?' Crescent asked without betraying any concern.

'As a brother I simply came here to apprise you of what is brewing in Delhi against your organization. If you do not take effective measures to stop your provocative acts, I suspect Delhi will start sealing the border more aggressively to prevent illegal immigrants from pouring in and your boys from sneaking in for terrorist purposes. It may also tell its friends in Dhaka that they will no longer be obliged to listen to us in dealing with you.'

'I don't understand why you are so bitterly opposed to illegal immigrants. Are they not contributing to your economy by providing services at a much cheaper cost? In fact, you should be grateful to us for providing you with inexpensive and qualified labour to keep your homes and infrastructure growing,' Crescent argued.

'We are not against illegal immigrants per say but what we object to is your effort to use them for subversive purposes, encouraging them to interfere with our political process. Delhi believes that while Pakistan's unfinished agenda is the annexation of Jammu and Kashmir, your unfinished agenda is to extend the boundary of Bangladesh westward and to

convert large areas of Bengal, Bihar, Assam and Tripura to your radical Islamic ideology,' Sujal said.

'These are idle beliefs and far from reality,' Crescent countered. 'Anyway, give me some time to think about what you have said and discuss it with the other leaders.'

'I think Sujal-da has made a sensible offer,' Shariful, who had kept silent so far, spoke up. 'If we don't build bridges with India and their pro-liberation friends here, our alleged genocidal role in the liberation war will certainly be used by the League to annihilate us, should they return to power. There is no guarantee that the Nationalists or the army will rule forever or continue to back us. Under the circumstances, we should profess our support to all parties based on issues, gradually reduce our anti-India rhetoric and refrain from being perceived as ISI's allies.'

Sujal was surprised at his friend's sudden burst of support. However, Crescent had different ideas.

'It is not easy for us to snap our historical ties with Jamaat-e-Islami of Pakistan or the Nationalist Party here. It is also naive to dream of working together with the League.'

Hossain did not press his point further.

'I will, nevertheless, wait for your response,' Sujal said, concluding the discussion.

Crescent stood up and shook hands with Sujal, saying that he looked forward to meeting him in less combative circumstances.

Shariful went to see off Crescent, showing him out through the back door to prevent his meeting Rehena. He was afraid that once Rehena met him and the conversation began, it would be difficult to stop her from forcing Crescent to stay for dinner. He wanted the seriousness of

the discussion to sink in on Crescent, and he was looking forward to spending some time with Sujal, whom he was meeting after a long time.

Meanwhile, Sujal went into the living room and waited for Shariful. Rehena joined him and wasted no time in firing off a series of questions about Arpita and the children and what they had all been doing since they had last seen each other. After Shariful returned, she declared that she wanted to invite a few of their common friends for dinner as well, but Shariful wouldn't agree and insisted on keeping it a private affair. Relieved, Sujal looked at him and smiled a silent thanks.

As usual, Rehena was a great hostess. Chirpy and well informed, she kept the dinner lively and regaled Sujal with the gossip doing the rounds in Dhaka's social and business circles. Shariful tried occasionally to divert her to more sober subjects but failed miserably. At 1.00 a.m., Sujal finally excused himself, begging exhaustion.

As Shariful drove him back to the hotel, Sujal wondered, 'How do you manage to remain so calm and detached in spite of having a wife who is so lively, warm and gregarious?'

'It's easy. I seldom argue,' Shariful responded with a deadpan expression.

Sujal laughed before turning serious. 'Did Crescent say anything about our discussion?'

'He said that he had tolerated your allegations out of courtesy but found your arguments and veiled threats offensive. I seriously doubt that he will come back to you. But why have you suddenly woken up to these realities? Matters have been like this for years and will continue like this for several more,' Hossain averred.

'Crescent is a good friend. I wanted to at least try and make him understand the folly of antagonizing both a powerful neighbour and the League,' Sujal said.

'I am not sure if you will ever be successful in preventing the entry of illegal immigrants or militants into India. It is not only Jamaat but your own officials, security forces and politicians who will ensure that this problem festers. I doubt Crescent will be able to convince the leadership and cadre to accept your terms.'

'Then let it be a failed mission. My brief was to convey Delhi's concerns to Crescent, which I have done. What happens now is not my worry. I am happy that as a bonus of this assignment, I was able to meet you and Rehena and enjoy your hospitality,' Sujal said as Shariful pulled up outside the hotel.

'Do you remember Mizan, my nephew, who is an immigration officer?' Shariful suddenly asked as they both stood on the pavement to say goodbye.

'Yes, of course,' Sujal responded, wary.

'He called me this afternoon to tell me that he had seen you at the airport. He asked whether I knew how to contact you. He checked the immigration records, but your name wasn't listed. Actually, he wants to visit the Ajmer Sharif Dargah, but his visa application has been stalled at the Indian High Commission. He wanted your help in getting it cleared,' Hossain said.

'You can note down his particulars and send them to me. But what did you tell him?'

'What else could I say other than deny any knowledge of your arrival?' Shariful replied, smiling.

Relieved, Sujal laughed as both shook hands and parted.

Eleven hours later, Sujal flew from Dhaka to Delhi.

A deafening silence prevailed as the tape of Sujal's conversation with Crescent, recorded secretly by him, finished playing. The Chief appeared disturbed as he gazed thoughtfully out of the window. Reddy was amazed at the officer's courage in taking on a hostile target in such a forthright manner. Vijay was relieved that Sujal had returned safely after playing the role of peacemaker. He was confident that the Chief would no longer question his insistence on assigning Sujal to the mission.

'I must commend you for bringing our concerns to Crescent's notice without beating about the bush,' the Chief told Sujal, breaking the silence. 'But your visit has rendered the project redundant. The cover of secrecy has been blown to bits. Crescent will definitely see your hand behind any attacks on his facilities and blame us for indulging in terrorist attacks. You should have avoided the trip if you wished to mount the operation.'

'Sir, both Vijay and Mr Reddy were opposed to my idea of going to Dhaka and agreed only on my insistence. I thought it would be worthwhile to try and avoid a bloody and costly operation, which is why I wanted to apprise Crescent of our stand regarding Jamaat's hostile activities and sound him out on whether he would be willing to accommodate our security concerns,' Sujal said.

'I appreciate your efforts and it's good to know Crescent's thoughts on the matter, but you can no longer execute this project without being exposed. I think you've effectively killed Vijay's proposal,' the Chief remarked with a grim face.

'Sir, I gave no indication of our plan to attack his facilities,' Sujal asserted. 'He can at best speculate about our complicity which, frankly, he should. That will unnerve him. It will also make him understand that next time no one will attempt to reason with him before destroying his staging camps and training units.'

'Let's not do anything till we hear back from Crescent.'

'Sir, we must not lose time. The sense I got was that Crescent and his cadres will not back down. Since we have agreed in principle to disrupt Jamaat's hostile activities, we should go ahead and plan the execution of the operation on the ground.'

'Reddy will inform you about our decision after we have had a chance to consider the options,' the Chief said, hinting that the meeting was over.

As the three officers stood up to leave, the Chief requested Reddy to remain.

'Vijay has handed you a terrible infant to manage,' the Chief said in jest, once the others had left. 'But he is indeed very different from other officers. I wish I had known him before. I could have used him in a couple of my operations that went awry in the hands of officers who were too hesitant.'

'This is my first experience as well in handling an officer who is so dangerously confident.'

'I notice that he has a tendency to take extraordinary risks. That is something that you will have to constantly watch. And don't let him visit Dhaka again for this purpose. Vijay and you may have to monitor his execution of the project closely, without appearing to be interfering. My impression is that if we advise him too much, he may clam up and withdraw.'

'Please don't worry,' Reddy assured him. 'It sounds like you're willing to give this mission the go-ahead.'

'Yes, but keep me in the loop. I'm very interested to see how he handles this operation.'

After Reddy returned to his room, he rang up Vijay and asked him to come to his office along with Sujal. As they walked to Reddy's office, Vijay surmised that the Chief, upset by Sujal's visit to Dhaka and wary of its potential consequences on the operation, had scrapped the project. Sujal, however, appeared unfazed.

They had barely sat down when Reddy broke the news that the Chief had cleared the mission but wanted to ensure that no footprint was left behind. Both officers looked at each other, Vijay feeling relieved and Sujal pleasantly surprised.

'Sir, I do not plan to involve any employee or asset of the Agency. My idea is to engage persons who have never been used by the Agency so that our complicity is not exposed,' Sujal clarified.

'Are they your old contacts?'

'No, sir, they are men whom I used for unofficial purposes.'

'If they are not trained, how will they carry out their respective tasks?

'Sir, novices are more daring and less demanding.'

'How much money do you expect to pay them?'

'It will be a sizeable sum, amounting to a couple of crores in all probability.'

'I don't think the project is worth investing so much,' Reddy responded, a worried look on his face.

Vijay, sitting quiet, was not surprised by this. He was familiar with Sujal's habit of paying much higher than other

operatives for a job in order to earn the swift and absolute loyalty of his assets. Sujal did not believe in negotiating and went straight for the jugular. An accountant's nightmare, he usually paid generous sums to secure his sources and did not waste time in cultivating them. Little wonder then that he ran his operations at a breakneck pace.

'Sir, in that case, we should shelve the mission. There is no point in wasting resources in a losing venture,' Sujal said.

Although Reddy did not appreciate Sujal's stance, he didn't let his displeasure show. 'Give me a detailed estimate of the likely expenditure. We will see what we can do,' he said.

'Sir, I will send you the estimate within a few weeks, after talking to my men in the field. If you find it unreasonable, please drop the mission.'

'It is premature to talk about abandoning the project,' Reddy responded, 'but your guess seems extravagant. I am not convinced that such a large sum will be necessary.'

'Sir, the amount I am asking for is actually peanuts. I have executed missions that were far more expensive.'

'Be that as it may, submit the estimate as soon as possible so that I can discuss it with the Chief and see whether he is willing to sanction the amount without any cuts.'

'Sir, I will need to go to Calcutta to hold initial discussions with my agents. I will need at least five lakhs to meet their expenses,' Sujal said.

'Very well, I will give you an advance today itself to meet your expenses.'

'Sir.'

'And one more thing. The Chief does not want you to visit Dhaka again,' Reddy cautioned.

'Sir, you can assure the Chief that I will do no such thing. As for the estimate of the likely expenditure, if needed, I will come personally to explain where and how I am going to spend the money.'

'That sounds reasonable to me,' Vijay said.

Reddy nodded his agreement. 'Anything else?'

'Sir, I need your assurance that if the mission is aborted, I will be relocated to Hyderabad.'

'I cannot guarantee that you will be relocated to Hyderabad because we cannot keep that position vacant for long, but I will certainly have you transferred from Calcutta,' Reddy assured him.

As there was nothing more to discuss, he took out an envelope from his safe and handed it to Sujal. It contained two lakh rupees. Sujal thanked him and both he and Vijay left Reddy's office.

As they walked towards the lift, Vijay remarked, 'I'm beginning to feel sorry for you, Sujal. You have now tried twice to wriggle out of this mission, first by taking a secret trip to Dhaka and then by asking for an astronomical amount to accomplish it, but failed on both counts.'

'There must be something about your project that keeps pulling me back,' Sujal replied, smiling. 'Let's just hope the Chief can find the money for it.'

Atul Kulkarni, head of the Agency's unit in Calcutta, missed a heartbeat as he read through a cable from headquarters. It conveyed the order transferring Sujal Rath from Hyderabad to Calcutta as his deputy. His first impulse was to call the Chief and protest, but better sense prevailed and he decided to wait till he knew all the facts behind the order. He opted

to call Vijay instead to try and discover the reason behind the transfer.

Vijay, however, pleaded ignorance. 'It's a routine matter,' he said. 'Someone had to fill in the vacancy after the previous deputy left. Maybe the Chief decided to post Sujal to the Calcutta desk because he served earlier in Bangladesh.'

'Has he worked under Reddy before?' Atul pressed for some clarity.

'I don't think so, but how does it matter? He is not going as Reddy's envoy but as your deputy. Why are you so worked up over his posting?' Vijay enquired.

'I'm concerned because he is a very difficult subordinate and always tries to run down his seniors.'

Not wishing to continue the conversation, Vijay hurriedly told him that he was being summoned by Reddy and hung up.

Over the next couple of days, Atul fretted over the order. His experience of working with Sujal had been anything but pleasant. He had found Sujal overly secretive and in the habit of going over the heads of his reporting officers in operational matters. While it was true that Sujal had a knack for picking up sources that Atul found difficult to even approach, he felt Sujal had a tendency to brag about his achievements and dismiss those of others, which infuriated him. But perhaps what annoyed Atul the most was Sujal's penchant for arguing, his casual approach to office administration and accounts and his total disinterest in analysing reports. Atul also did not like or trust his large circle of contacts, most of whom were either from the business world or had dubious backgrounds. As upset as he was by the order, Atul eventually decided not to take the matter up with headquarters, consoling himself with the

thought that he was unlikely to stay in Calcutta long since he was due for an assignment abroad in the next few months.

Sujal arrived in Calcutta to a frosty welcome. A rickety jeep was sent to fetch him from Dum Dum airport and drive him to the Agency's guesthouse in Ulta Danga, which had no cooking facilities. The driver informed him that Mr Kulkarni was on a tour of inspection and would return after three or four days. Sujal was not surprised. He was familiar with Atul's pettiness. He knew that dealing with him would not be easy. Atul derived pleasure in running him down for 'writing poorly and speaking incoherently'. Moreover, Atul's habit of constantly inquiring about his movements and meetings with his assets and his insistence on seeing all his reports irked him. Worse, Atul suffered from such a sense of insecurity that he would often call for Sujal's phone bills behind his back to check whom he was talking to at headquarters and then demand the details of what had transpired.

In spite of their mutual animosity, both managed to maintain a civil working relationship for the first few days. But the unspoken truce did not last long. When Reddy sent a cable summoning Sujal to headquarters for consultations, Atul lost his cool.

'What is going on behind my back? Why is he summoning you and not me?' he confronted Sujal.

'You are asking the wrong person. Why don't you speak to Mr Reddy?' Sujal responded, unruffled.

Atul didn't back down. 'Did you check with Vijay why his boss has asked for you?'

'No. I don't make a habit of verifying the motives behind an order from my senior. Perhaps Mr Reddy doesn't want Vijay to know about our meeting.'

Atul frowned. 'Did you visit headquarters to receive a briefing from Mr Reddy regarding your assignment in Calcutta?' Atul asked, recalling his fleeting encounter with his deputy in the lift some weeks ago.

'I did meet him, but there was no discussion about the assignment. He merely told me that I should be ready to be posted to Calcutta as your deputy and to wait for further instructions. In fact, I protested my transfer from Hyderabad, but neither he nor the Chief would listen. I told him about my wife's slow recovery after her surgery but it made no difference. In fact, I would be grateful if you could get my posting cancelled,' Sujal said with a straight face, leaving Atul groping for a suitable response.

That same evening Sujal left for Delhi.

At headquarters, Sujal gave Reddy a detailed presentation on his mission plan, listing the areas that he was planning to target, confirming the amount of service money he would need, sharing information on the types of persons he would be recruiting to help him execute the project and the safety measures he would be adopting. Reddy listened intently, and apart from a few clarifications regarding minor details, he did not question Sujal on any major aspect of the plan. Instead, he said that with Sujal in charge of the operation, he felt that he did not have to worry about its execution or any exposure. He also hinted that Atul would soon be recalled to headquarters, leaving Sujal as the virtual head of the Calcutta unit to run his Jamaat operation in the manner he liked.

Business concluded, both Reddy and Sujal relaxed and Reddy invited Sujal to have dinner with him. He also gave

Sujal permission to spend a few days in Hyderabad with his family before returning to Calcutta.

Feeling refreshed after meeting his wife and children and happy about the unqualified support promised by Reddy for his plan, Sujal threw himself into the task of re-establishing contact with his network in Bangladesh and Calcutta. He knew he would need their help in identifying and selecting people for the project.

Atul, meanwhile, waited anxiously for Sujal to bring him to speed about what he had discussed with Reddy in Delhi, but his deputy remained silent on the subject. Finally, running out of patience, he summoned Sujal for a meeting.

'How did your meeting in Delhi go?' he began.

'It wasn't very productive. Neither Vijay nor Reddy gave me a clear idea of what I am supposed to do here. I was supposed to meet the Chief to discuss the matter, but he was called away on urgent business and I wasn't able to meet him,' Sujal replied.

'But they must have given you some idea of why they have sent you here. I'm sure Reddy didn't call you all the way to headquarters just to entertain you.'

'Actually, he did exactly that. He took me out for dinner and permitted me to visit my wife in Hyderabad.'

Seething with anger by now, Atul asked, 'How long have you known Reddy?'

'I had a chance meeting with him only last month when he mentioned that he would like me to assist him in a high-level operation and that I might have to visit headquarters frequently for this purpose,' Sujal informed him casually.

Atul was furious. He suspected that his deputy was playing games with him and conspiring behind his back, but it seemed there was not much he could do about it. His suspicion was confirmed when a week later, he was transferred to headquarters, leaving Sujal to manage the Agency's unit in Calcutta independently.

Sujal had never had it so good. He was allotted a nice government accommodation in Alipore. Arpita and the children soon moved to Calcutta to join him. The change of place brought about a sea change in her health and she began feeling stronger with each passing day. The kids too were happy—they were attending a good public school and making friends who spoke their language and ate their kind of food.

As for Sujal, with no one to dictate terms and interfere, he had the freedom to contact his trusted talent spotters in Bangladesh and his old associates in Dhaka, Chittagong, Rajshahi and Khulna. He asked them to send him the names of volunteers whom he could trust for a special project. Within a fortnight, he had a list of thirty-five names. From these, he selected five whom he had used earlier to carry out a couple of secret assignments for the Indian High Commissioner to Bangladesh and to facilitate the transfer of arms and explosives for his friends in the League to aid their cadres in Jamaat strongholds. To assist him in handling the logistics of the operation, he selected field operative Saumen Bose of the Calcutta unit, whom he found to be loyal, hardworking, discreet and extremely knowledgeable about the Bangladeshis in the city.

Once the names of the assets were finalized, Sujal called each one of them to set up meetings in Calcutta on different dates. As per his plan, Saumen would help the volunteers enter India illegally through the Ghojadanga check post in Basirhat in West Bengal, and then escort them to Calcutta, where they would be put up in different hotels, depending on which ones were more secure and less frequented by the local police. Sujal would meet the visitors, discuss their individual roles and ask them for their views on the feasibility of their tasks and the difficulties that they could face in executing them. Based on their inputs, he would work out the details of the operation that he named simply as 'Mission'.

Events moved rapidly thereafter. Within ten days, the assets began to arrive. Sujal met them, briefed them and allotted them their specific tasks. He ensured that they did not stay longer than absolutely necessary, lest they attracted the attention of the Intelligence Bureau and the watchers of Calcutta police. His asset Aziz was assigned the responsibility of reconnoitering the Jamaat and HuJI posts, their training facilities and madrasas along the border and in other parts of Bangladesh and drawing up a list of their precise locations. Mansoor was to identify volunteers who would carry out the assault. Shaukat, a greedy but highly resourceful asset, was entrusted with the task of procuring explosives from his sources. Mortaza was told to make arrangements for the delivery of the explosives to the marked locations. Each one was to specify how much money he would need to execute his task. The last man Sujal briefed was Israr. He was to play the role of coordinator and remain in Dhaka during the entire operation to deal with unforeseen problems at short notice. Israr was quick to sense what was in the offing. Being

a die-hard League supporter, he hated Jamaat and urged Sujal to widen the scope of the operation, so as to really make it count in its impact, and even offered to involve his own men in punishing 'the rogues' beyond recovery in the foreseeable future. Sujal advised restraint and cautioned him against doing anything rash that might harm the secrecy of the mission.

All the assets were also advised to contact Sujal either in person or from designated PCOs and never through mobile phones. The purpose of the mission was not disclosed to anyone except Israr. Nor were they told who else was involved in the project. Most of the men accepted their roles without probing for further details beyond what was required to carry out their respective tasks. Only Shaukat was inquisitive. He wanted to know where the explosives were being sent and who the consignee was. Sujal advised him not to ask too many questions and to focus on what he was going to receive in return for this job, rather than on details that did not concern him. Knowing where his real interest lay, he offered Shaukat 10 per cent of the actual cost of the total shipment as his facilitation fees, which could be in lakhs. Shaukat couldn't believe his luck and realized he had more to gain by his silence.

A day after Israr, the last of the agents, was pushed across the border, Saumen met Sujal at the latter's residence. 'Sir, I don't have any idea about the real objective of this mission,' he began cautiously, 'which is why I feel neither excited about it nor involved. In fact, handling these Bangladeshis makes me nervous.'

'Did anyone threaten you?' Sujal asked.

'No, sir. But everything about them was strange. They rarely spoke unless absolutely necessary, they neither ate nor

drank during the journey to Calcutta, perhaps suspicious of what I would feed them. They also seemed in a hurry to return home. They were so different from the sources I have worked with so far,' Saumen confessed.

Realizing that Saumen had much to learn about dealing with all variety of assets, Sujal chose to allay his concerns by commending him for the way he had handled them.

'You dealt with the situation well, Saumen. More surprises are awaiting you as the mission gets under-way. But I bet you will enjoy having pulled it off in the end.'

Arpita, who had been quietly listening to the discussion, intervened to calm Saumen's nerves.

'Your boss has an awful habit of keeping everyone guessing and seldom shares his antics even with his wife,' she said. 'But you need not worry. If he has picked you for a job, he won't let you down. On the contrary, you may learn a few tricks along the way.'

Saumen found it unusual for an intelligence officer's wife to arbitrate in operational matters but guessed that, like Sujal, she was also probably different from the other Agency wives.

Later that night, after Sujal had gone to bed, Arpita lay quietly next to him, thinking about the past few weeks. She had not seen him this happy and relaxed in the past four years. Every evening when he returned home, he would excitedly tell her whom he had contacted in Dhaka, how he was approaching the mission and ask her to point out the flaws in the plan as an outsider. She noticed that with each passing day, he was becoming increasingly convinced that the mission would be a success.

Arpita's sense of the situation, however, was a bit premature. Sujal's enthusiasm took a beating when Prabhakar Dayal, a voluble officer filled with a sense of his own self-importance, arrived in Calcutta to take over the position held by Atul Kulkarni. Dayal had a high opinion of his skills as an ace operator and believed that senior officers unfairly criticized his suggestions as irrelevant and his ideas as scattered. It was not possible for him to be cogent and precise when discussing a subject. A poor administrator, he could seldom take a decision as he got bogged down with needless clerical details. He derived pleasure in undercutting his junior colleagues and did not mind ruining their career to project himself as a paragon of professional virtue. However, what stood him in good stead was his capacity to suffer humiliation to keep his bosses on his right side. Though Sujal had not served under him before, he was apprehensive. He had heard from Vijay that Dayal was mean and vengeful, lacked the ability to plan a feasible operation and was a veteran at ambushing his rivals to stay close to the top leadership.

Within a few days, Sujal realized that unlike Atul Kulkarni, Dayal would neither question him about his project nor interfere, but he would not be cooperative either. It was apparent that he had been fully briefed by Atul on Sujal's involvement in a high-level operation and his proximity to Vishwanath Reddy.

'I believe Mr Reddy has assigned you to an operation. Execute it on a priority basis,' he told Sujal. 'If you perform well, you can go places. Reddy can easily have you assigned to a lucrative station abroad. I'm sure you know that he is the Chief's closest confidant at headquarters,' he paused to sign

a paper brought in by his assistant. Sujal waited patiently, observing Dayal's modus operandi.

'Don't worry about the unit's administrative and operational work,' Dayal continued after his assistant had left. 'I will take care of it until you have completed the assignment entrusted to you by Mr Reddy. Depending on how much time you can spare from his operation, I will allocate the work between the two of us.'

Sujal had heard enough about Dayal to know not to take his words at face value. He didn't doubt that behind the façade of a reasonable boss was someone who wouldn't hesitate to undercut and sabotage him. Sujal therefore kept quiet, thinking it best to avoid saying anything that might later be used against him.

'I understand you have to make frequent trips to Delhi in connection with Mr Reddy's project. Keep me informed of your travel plans in advance so that I can make arrangements to ensure that the routine work of the unit does not suffer,' Dayal instructed him.

Not wishing to prolong the meeting, Sujal agreed and left.

The real blow, however, came when Sujal heard that Vijay had been transferred from headquarters. He was to be replaced by Amit Prasad. Amit had been junior to him when they had joined the service. However, Sujal's career had stalled over the years due to his style of working, which bred jealousy and anger among his colleagues and seniors, while Amit had quietly moved up the ladder, unnoticed. They had remained mere acquaintances through the years. With Vijay gone, Sujal had no one with whom he could discuss matters freely and receive, in turn, measured advice and support. He suspected that his proximity to Reddy

would be frowned upon by both Dayal and Amit privately, but he felt he would be able to handle their pettiness. He had worked before in more unfavourable circumstances and had managed to survive, largely because his operations succeeded and he had been lucky to have chiefs who had supported him throughout. This time also, with the Chief and Reddy on his side, he saw no reason why he could not pull off the mission regardless of how many roadblocks Dayal raised. He did think briefly about speaking to Reddy regarding the postings of Amit and Dayal but dropped the idea, believing that it might reflect poorly on his ability to work with different kinds of people. He could not possibly find fault with headquarters just because he disliked Amit and Dayal.

As if sensing his predicament, Reddy called Sujal a couple of days later.

'I am sure you have concerns regarding working with Amit and Dayal,' he said. 'Don't worry. Vijay handed over all the material related to the mission to me. I have, meanwhile, instructed Amit to deal only with Dayal and to leave you alone. I have also informed Dayal that the Chief has given you a job for which you will be required to visit Delhi frequently.'

'Sir, couldn't headquarters find more suitable officers to fill these posts?' Sujal asked after some hesitation.

'I guess they couldn't. These are routine administrative decisions and I generally do not get involved in them,' Reddy remarked and then asked if he had any news from his boys.

'Not yet, but they still have a week to meet the deadline. I have no doubt I'll be hearing from them soon,' Sujal said.

'Keep me informed,' Reddy said before hanging up.

The feedback from the agents was encouraging. Aziz was able to procure valuable information on Jamaat's launching posts along the Bangladesh side of the border, their training camps in various parts of the country and the locations of safe houses in and around Dhaka where ISI briefed militants and from where Jamaat took them to facilitate their infiltration into India. He and Sujal spent several hours poring over maps, plotting the various locations, working out the distances between them and identifying prominent landmarks so that the assault group did not have any problems in finding and approaching the targets.

Sujal paid him 75,000 taka for his efforts. When he informed Reddy about the intelligence gained from Aziz, Reddy's response was lukewarm.

'Much of this data has been provided by Vijay in his proposal. I see no value addition here, and definitely no need to pay so much for such routine information,' Reddy said with a hint of annoyance.

'Sir, the information in Vijay's report is outdated; at best it is inexact and in most cases, it is wrong. A mission of this sensitivity cannot be launched on the basis of guesswork,' Sujal stressed. 'As for Aziz's fee, given the quality of the information, it is reasonable, and moreover, it is far below his ask. In fact, I wanted to pay him more but couldn't as I must keep enough funds for the other assets.'

'Very well, it seems that you do know what you are doing,' Reddy conceded. 'I will release the remaining amount shortly.'

Relieved that Reddy didn't feel the need to grill him further, Sujal turned his attention to more pressing matters.

Mansoor had arrived with a list of nine volunteers who would carry out the assaults on the ground. Well aware of how important it was to know one's team, Sujal asked Mansoor for detailed information on each volunteer—their family profile, age, financial expectations and more importantly, their motivation. The agent sought five lakh taka for each of his boys and three lakhs for himself in addition to the ten lakhs that he would need to take care of the injured and dead. Even by his generous standards, Sujal found the demand unreasonably high.

'I am aware of the grave risk that your boys will be exposed to, but it will be difficult for me to raise so much money. Have you already promised them this fee?' he asked.

'No.'

'That's good. Please check with me before committing any amount.'

'But you have to give me some idea of how much you can pay. They are not going to work out of love for your mission.'

'Give me some time to work out an approximate figure; keep in mind, though, that it will be far less than your expectations. Anyway, what did you tell the boys about what they have to do?'

'I explained that they might be required to destroy a few offices in return for generous payments. They have no interest in knowing more about the job as long as they are paid well.'

'Do they know each other?'

'No. I met them separately.'

'Good. This is what I like about you. You think of everything. I cannot think of anyone better when it comes to executing the most critical aspects of an operation,' Sujal

said appreciatively. He handed him 90,000 taka. 'I will send more in a few days,' he added.

Mansoor then asked Sujal to note down the telephone numbers of two PCOs where he could be reached.

'Will your boys have a problem with my choice of the targets?' Sujal asked.

'I don't think so. But what exactly is the target?'

'I will let you know in due course,' Sujal said.

'When will the material be available to carry out the damage?'

'I will let you know when it has been delivered. When we talk on the phone, we will refer to the explosives as apples,' Sujal said and then handed him a laminated card with the number 4pYrX4 and a symbol of a half-moon on it. 'Keep this safely with you. You and the man responsible for the apples will show one another the identical card to establish that both of you are meeting the right person.'

'Who is this man?'

'He is the one who will provide the material,' Sujal replied. 'You will be contacted when the time is right. Mansoor, you have done good work. Our business is done for now; be ready to leave after dinner. Saumen will escort you to the border.'

The next asset to arrive was Shaukat.

'I have identified three sources from whom I will be procuring the material you requested,' Shaukat informed Sujal.

'Good. It's better to use multiple sources. How much do they want?'

'A minimum of fifty lakhs, and they are insisting on full payment before the delivery, to be made over six to seven days. They want a detailed list of the items required, as well

as quantities. And they need a fortnight's notice to procure the material.'

'I will give you the list tomorrow,' Sujal promised. 'Where will you store the material?'

'Don't worry, I know of a place where we can keep the material, no questions asked, no problem. All I need from you is the name of the consignee.'

'I will soon be making arrangements for the consignee to meet you in person in Dhaka,' Sujal said, handing him a card identical to the one that he had given Mansoor earlier. 'Make sure that he shows you the same card before discussing anything.'

'So, the material is going to be used in my country. What are you actually up to? Are you going to target the Nationalists or your insurgents?' Shaukat enquired.

'I don't know about the target as of now. It is quite possible that the material will not be used in your country. The person whom you have to meet is just a courier.'

Taking the hint, Shaukat refrained from asking any further questions. Instead, he gave Sujal a short list of numbers on which he could be contacted in an emergency.

The following day, Saumen gave Shaukat the comprehensive list of 'material' required, duly vetted by an explosives expert. Armed with the information, Shaukat returned to Bangladesh via a covert route, aided by Saumen.

Sujal flew to Delhi the following day to update Reddy and to secure the next tranche of service money. He would need at least three crores at his disposal. Familiar with Reddy's way of operating by now, he had drawn up a detailed break-up of the expenses and a timetable for the mission's execution.

Reddy read through Sujal's notes carefully. He appreciated Sujal's attention to detail and the manner in which he had clearly defined each asset's responsibilities and drawn up a schedule of all mission-related activities.

'It is incredible what you have accomplished in five weeks. I'm beginning to believe that you will actually pull this off,' Reddy said with a smile. 'However, since the Chief is out of station, the monetary approval may have to wait for a few days.'

'Sir, do you anticipate any problems in sanctioning the requested amount?' Sujal enquired.

'What you're asking for is not a small sum. And given the Agency's track record of being penny wise and pound foolish, it won't be easy to organize this amount. But the Chief is a sensible man. I am confident he will clear the request, especially given the excellent work you have done so far and all the preparations you have made.'

However, the days passed with no further news from Reddy. Sujal became increasingly worried by the long silence, and when Reddy finally called after almost a month, asking him to come to Delhi, he hinted that the project might have to be aborted. Fuming, Sujal seriously considered not going to Delhi, feigning sickness, but he realized that if the mission was to be scrapped, he should take this opportunity to remind Reddy of his promise to transfer him from Calcutta. He also wanted to know what had prompted Reddy to take a U-turn. Was it the money that he was asking for, the fear of exposure or their lack of confidence in his capacity to deliver? Arpita counselled him to accept Reddy's decision gracefully and not to press for his transfer from Calcutta, at least for the sake of the children and her health.

Sujal landed in Delhi the following day and went straight to the office to meet Reddy.

'I know you will be unhappy to hear this,' Reddy began on a sombre note, 'but there is a view that this mission is becoming too expensive. Further, there is talk about making a fresh attempt to pressure Crescent into closing down his staging posts along the border. If he does not agree, vigilance by security forces and the intelligence agencies along our side of the border will be tightened to prevent illegal immigrants and militants from entering India.'

'Sir, it was never on your agenda to drill sense into Crescent or step up surveillance along the border,' Sujal reminded him. 'But if you feel that the mission has to be abandoned, please transfer me to another desk in western India. If I stay on in Calcutta, my contacts will no doubt try to seek me out and ask why I am scrapping the project. Sir, they know that I never give up once an operation is set in motion. I obviously cannot tell them that headquarters has had a change of heart or that it has run short of funds.'

'Let's not get ahead of ourselves; I have not yet decided to pull you out,' Reddy responded. 'While Vijay was here, it was easier to follow up with you on the mission. But with Vijay gone and my own busy schedule, I don't get the time to focus on this mission. I did suggest to the Chief that we leave this operation entirely in your hands, but he wouldn't agree. He insists that I closely monitor its execution, lest you become too adventurous.'

Sujal sensed that Reddy was not speaking the whole truth. Neither Vijay nor Reddy had ever contributed to or amended his plan of action or shown any interest in monitoring any mission of his. They simply wanted to

know how the operation was shaping up. So, why had this need for monitoring arisen all of a sudden, he wondered.

'Sir, why don't I write a note on your behalf, arguing that this mission is not feasible and fraught with adverse consequences for our bilateral relations? I can also highlight the flaws in the plan of action and how these could undermine our anonymity. I am sure the Chief would be happy to endorse the arguments to get rid of me and the mission.' Sujal's voice dripped with sarcasm.

'No, there's no need for that.' Reddy sighed. 'Back in the day, our approach to critical operations was not so bureaucratic and cautious. But things have changed for the worse.'

Sujal remained silent.

After a contemplative pause, Reddy went on. 'I'm not rethinking the mission,' Reddy assured him. 'My problem is the Chief. He continuously shifts his goal posts. One day he is enthusiastic about the mission, but the next day, he worries about its adverse fallout. He believes that if violence is unleashed on this magnitude, various political and religious groups will get sucked into no-holds-barred clashes, causing immense suffering to the League activists and particularly to Hindus.'

'Wasn't all this discussed with him before you summoned me to take up this assignment?'

'It was, but even at that stage, he was reluctant to accept Vijay's proposal. His biggest problem lies in providing the required funds without letting anyone know about it. He fears that the withdrawal of such large sums of money without any paperwork might be questioned later and motives could be attributed after all of us exit from the scene. He therefore wants you to reduce the expenditure by

75 per cent and plan payments to your agents over a period of six months.'

'Sir, let's just call it off,' Sujal snapped.

'I didn't peg you as one to give up so easily.' Reddy sounded surprised.

'Sir, if you remember, I had asked for three assurances before agreeing to the mission. The first was that no one should waver or scrap the operation once it is under way, or curtail its scope. The second was that if there were any difficulties in making available the required resources, I should be informed before the start of the operation.'

'I remember. And we agreed to your terms in good faith. But circumstances are forcing us to rethink things. Besides, you know how difficult it can be to apportion large sums for such unlisted operations.'

Sujal was quiet for a moment before responding. 'I can still do it, but not with 25 per cent of the estimated budget. That's not even enough to take Crescent out for dinner.'

Reddy laughed. 'By how much can you cut it down?'

'Sir, in such operations payments are made in advance to field operatives, for no one knows how things will pan out and who will survive the day to receive their share. In any case, the full amount will have to be paid to the asset before he starts procuring the material.'

'Leaving aside the amount required for the moment, once the money has been transferred, how can you be sure that your assets won't go back on their word or simply vanish? I don't think it's a good idea to pay the full amount in advance to anyone.' Reddy said.

'Sir, I have always operated on trust and I have not been betrayed so far.'

'Why don't you send me a revised estimate of the expenditure, at least for my sake?' Reddy asked. 'Bring it down to preferably a third of the original cost. If you need more, I will provide it from my resources without keeping the Chief in the picture.'

'Sir, I have never undertaken a mission half-heartedly but since you insist, I will give it a try,' Sujal said, sounding doubtful.

Reddy suspected that he would not submit a pruned budget.

With nothing further to discuss, Sujal took his leave and headed to the airport to catch his flight to Calcutta.

The flight to Calcutta took off on time. Once the seat belt sign was switched off, Sujal loosened the belt, pushed his seat back and stretched. Feeling mentally exhausted, he closed his eyes and tried to sleep but failed, as he was too wound up after his meeting. Reddy's volte-face had upset him deeply. He wanted to walk out of the mission rather than curtail its scope and wondered what Jeevnathan would have liked him to do in these circumstances. He would have told him to execute it anyway, Sujal knew, with or without approval or assistance from Aulakh, so long as it secured India's security interests.

The odds were indeed stacked against him, but why not give it a try, Sujal reasoned. The worst that could happen was that the mission would fail and he would get a rap on his knuckles from the Chief for undertaking it in defiance of his instructions. But that was no big deal. He was used to taking such reverses in stride and moving on. The important thing to consider was from where the money required to complete the mission could be sourced. The Chief and Reddy were reluctant to provide the funds. So, from where could he get

the money? Funds had never been a problem for Jeevnathan. Being head of the unit, he had always had service money at his disposal, which he had juggled to pay for operations that headquarters did not approve of. But Sujal didn't have such access to service money. A thought struck him. What if he was able to raise the funds through private sources? He knew the idea was far-fetched, as such a thing had never been done before for an Agency operation, but perhaps he could find a way to make it work. However, would the Chief haul him up for approaching outsiders for money to run an intelligence operation, or would he be offended, as the move would reflect poorly on his leadership? Was there really any need to take such a risk and displease everyone? Why did he feel that the burden of preventing eastern India's demography from being distorted lay squarely on his shoulders? The questions kept running through his head until he eventually dozed off.

He reached home at around 11.00 p.m. to find Arpita waiting eagerly for his return to hear about the outcome of his visit. He didn't say much, going straight to the bedroom to change and have a quick wash. She sensed that something had gone wrong. While he was having a drink before his late dinner, she joined him.

'Did the Chief scrap the mission?' she asked as she sat down beside him.

'I couldn't meet him, but Reddy evidently seems to have lost interest. He wants me to believe that if he has his way, he will continue funding the mission, but the Chief is holding him back. I don't know whom to trust. He says he doesn't have the power to sanction the amount of service money that I need and has asked me to slash the budget,' Sujal said bitterly.

'Then do what he has advised. After all, this is his operation and surely he knows best whether to run it and how. I hope you didn't get angry and press for a transfer,' she enquired.

'Let him find an officer who will work at his bidding. I never asked for this job. It was thrust on me. I will undertake it only on my terms. I am not sending him any revised proposal. But don't worry, we won't leave Calcutta for another year,' Sujal said.

Realizing that Sujal was upset, Arpita wisely decided not to pursue the conversation further.

Sujal quickly finished his drink, had his dinner and retired to bed. But sleep eluded him. He lay awake in the dark and began shortlisting his friends and contacts who could finance the project. Suddenly, he remembered a person. He tossed and turned for the rest of the night, impatient for dawn to break so that he could go meet him.

The first thing that Sujal did in the morning was to shut himself in the garage and search for a diary containing his old Bangladeshi contacts among the stacks of paper lying in a disorganized state in cartons. He was looking for the phone numbers and addresses of one Mazhar and his leader Sahib who headed the People's Front in Bangladesh. He recalled that Mazhar had once mentioned to him that Sahib would pay him any amount if he could punish Jamaat for helping the Nationalists to incarcerate him.

After nearly four hours of searching, Sujal succeeded in locating a diary that contained Mazhar's contact information in Dhaka. He promptly left the house to call the numbers

from a nearby public phone booth but was told by the operator that they were no longer in service.

Undeterred, Sujal next called several contacts who he knew had links with Mazhar. One of them told him that Mazhar was no longer in Dhaka and had probably moved to India or Bangkok. Finally, it was the ever-dependable Israr who provided the breakthrough. He informed Sujal that Mazhar was hibernating somewhere in Calcutta, taking care of Sahib's financial and political interests with the help of his local Bangladeshi contacts. Sujal immediately instructed Saumen to track him down using his extensive knowledge of the illegal immigrants in the Park Circus and new Wakaf areas. It took Saumen only three days to locate the address and telephone numbers of Mazhar. Sujal wasted no time in calling him. He waited anxiously as the phone rang several times and just as he was about to give up hope, a man with a distinctive baritone answered. Sujal immediately recognized him as Mazhar.

'Hello, Mazhar bhai. This is Sujal Rath. I have recently been posted to Calcutta,' he said.

'What a surprise!' Mazhar said but did not sound particularly pleased to be hearing from him.

'Is it possible for us meet?' Sujal enquired. 'I know you must think that I let you down very badly. I wanted to come and explain what went wrong and why I couldn't fulfil my commitment given to Sahib.'

There was silence for a few seconds.

'Someone will contact you shortly,' Mazhar said and hung up. Having seen the workings of the National Security Intelligence from close quarters for years and conscious of its network of watchers in Calcutta, Mazhar was afraid of giving away any information about his location or

engaging in polite conversation about their past association on an open line.

The man who eventually came to see Sujal was Nurul Hassan, a businessman who, like Mazhar, was also on the run to evade arrest, warranted by a court in Dhaka for his involvement in alleged anti-state activities. Sujal knew Nurul from his days in Dhaka. He saw that he was still as chubby and charming as ever, although he had greyed at his temples. Sujal welcomed him warmly and apologized for remaining incommunicado for so long.

'I'm sure you had your reasons,' Nurul said and paused for a few seconds. 'For us, it has been a very difficult seven years,' he continued slowly. 'Soon after you left, Mazhar and I had to flee Dhaka after Sahib was detained by the Nationalists. Initially, we lay low, but once the search for us cooled off somewhat, we slowly began to invest in local businesses. Mazhar uses the dividends to bribe Bangladeshi officials to ensure that Sahib receives at least the basic comforts and the People's Front is kept afloat. I manage the police and municipal officials here so that we are not harassed for overstaying without proper documents.'

'Did Jamaat not put pressure on the Nationalists to treat Sahib with respect? How could they forget that Sahib was of tremendous help in expanding their cadre base and gaining political legitimacy?' Sujal enquired.

'They didn't lift a finger to help. In fact, they collaborated with the Nationalists in treating Sahib like a common criminal,' Nurul said bitterly.

Not keen on dwelling on the issue further, Sujal changed the topic, inquiring about Nurul's family.

'Chanda is with me in Calcutta and my two kids are in a boarding school in Ooty. Mazhar lives alone. His wife

remained in Dhaka with their son, and is looking after the family business there,' Nurul said, bringing him up to date.

'Is it possible to meet Mazhar?' Sujal asked, having done with the pleasantries.

'I have been asked to give you his home address and a telephone number.' Nurul scribbled the details on a piece of paper, which he handed to Sujal.

Sujal looked at it and noticed that the address was different from the one that Saumen's contacts had provided. He thanked Nurul, who told him that Mazhar would be waiting for him in his house in Baguihati on the following evening at nine.

The day of Sujal's encounter with Mazhar did not start on a propitious note. A religious man, Sujal had his share of superstitions, particularly when he embarked on a mission. As he was getting ready to leave for the office, he looked out of the window at the sky. It was overcast with dark clouds threatening to pour any moment. He waited for half an hour for the rain to fall and the skies to clear, but the clouds lingered ominously, and the rain never came. He thought it was a bad omen. Since he had to write a brief note on the project for Mazhar, explaining how it would benefit Sahib, he had no choice but to leave for the office. No sooner did he sit in his car than Reddy called on his cell phone.

'Sujal, I haven't heard from you in a while. Have you revised the mission plan and budget? I know I'm pushing you, but as the Chief is due to retire soon, he's keen on taking a decision one way or the other before the end of

the month so that if something goes wrong, he will still be around to control the damage.'

'Sir, I'm working on the revisions and will be in touch soon,' Sujal lied.

'Don't keep us waiting too long,' Reddy said before hanging up.

It was obvious that while the Chief approved of the mission in principle, he did not have the stomach to back it up fully. For Sujal, the project was as good as dead and his forthcoming meeting with Mazhar was just a gamble.

As soon as he walked into the office, his assistant informed him that Dayal was looking for him. Not looking forward to the encounter, Sujal headed to his office and found Dayal in a foul mood. The latter wasted no time in launching a litany of complaints against Sujal—his frequent absences from the office, and his unavailability for any other work of the unit. Realizing that there was nothing to be gained by arguing and unwilling to prolong the meeting any more than necessary, Sujal uttered a few placating words and made his escape.

Finally alone in his own office, he closed the door, told his assistant not to disturb him, switched off his cell phone and began writing the brief for Mazhar.

At 7.00 p.m., Sujal left for home in his official car. He had hardly covered a kilometre when the rain that had been threatening all day finally came down in torrents, accompanied by a strong wind. It wasn't long before he was caught in the inevitable traffic jam. He knew he would never make it to Mazhar's house by 9.00 p.m. if he went home first, so he decided to head directly to Mazhar's place. Keen to keep the meeting under wraps, he dismissed the Agency driver before jumping out of the car to hail a taxi.

It was 9.50 p.m. when the taxi finally pulled up in front of the house. Anxious because he was almost an hour late, Sujal quickly paid the fare and almost sprinted through the small wooden gate and up the short pathway to the front door. He rang the bell, and as he waited for someone to open the door, he looked around. It was a single-storey, independent house of fairly new construction. The lighting around the house was very poor. He had had difficulty in reading the house number, and had almost tripped when negotiating the few steps up to the front door. A few minutes later, he rang the bell again. This time, an elderly man opened the door. Sujal told him who he was and was led inside to a sprawling living room. Once he was seated on a large, plush sofa, Sujal asked if Mazhar was home. It was unusual for Mazhar, known for being an excellent host, to keep his guest waiting.

'He should be home soon. He is caught in a terrible traffic jam and has instructed me to look after you in his absence,' the old man said before withdrawing to bring Sujal some refreshments.

Mazhar finally returned at 10.25 p.m. He apologized profusely for the delay, cursing the inept management of traffic by the Calcutta metropolitan police, particularly during the rains.

'That's okay,' Sujal said and enquired how Sahib was doing. 'Does he still think that I betrayed him and did nothing to ensure his political rehabilitation?'

'I don't know where to begin. It was hell after you left Dhaka. The Nationalists threw Sahib in detention, a witch-hunt was started and several of our supporters were either killed or prosecuted on trumped-up charges. I managed to escape, thanks to Nurul's efforts and his timely warning.'

'How is Sahib's health?' Sujal asked.

'He is not well and moreover, he is bitter and disillusioned. Everyone stabbed him in the back,' Mazhar responded. 'The Nationalists and Jamaat, which had promised to provide him protection and facilities befitting his political standing, took a complete U-turn after forming the government and systematically tried to decimate his party. They have since dragged him to court on false charges of corruption, misuse of power and anti-national activities. Even you, who had promised to secure his dignity, chose to run away and remained untraceable. Do you remember? You always complained that when in power, Sahib did nothing to address India's security concerns, that he took no action to curb the anti-India activities of Jamaat and ISI. Why don't you now act against the Nationalists and Jamaat leaders who are spewing venom against your country and inciting their cadres to attack Hindus and their shrines in Bangladesh?'

'You have every right to be angry with me. I made those promises at the behest of my government. I later learnt that Delhi could not force the Nationalists to treat Sahib fairly. Perhaps I could have still done something, but I was not in India,' Sujal said defensively.

Mazhar said nothing and after a brief but tense silence, excused himself. He returned soon, carrying two glasses of whisky. Accepting a glass and recognizing it for what it signalled—a suspension of hostilities—Sujal relaxed a little. Slowly, the tension eased and both began exchanging memories of the good old times and news on each other's families. Dinner was served by the old man and after a hearty meal, they retired to the living room once again. As Mazhar poured liquor into two glasses, Sujal told him that he had come to discuss something very serious.

'I guessed as much,' Mazhar responded, handing Sujal a glass.

'Do you recall you came to me once with an offer from Sahib to pay any amount to secure his freedom and have his privileges, including proper government accommodation, security and freedom of movement both within and outside the country, restored?' Sujal asked.

'I do.'

'I have a plan to avenge his humiliation. The idea is to take on Jamaat and force them to unleash mayhem in the country. This is bound to provoke a sharp reaction from the League, which will no doubt lead to an alarming deterioration in the law and order situation. Once that happens, the Nationalists, being partners of Jamaat in the government, are likely to come under enormous pressure to step down or drop Jamaat. They may not be left with any choice but to seek support from other parties, barring the League of course, to remain in power. That will be the time when Sahib can ask for his pound of flesh and demand the restoration of his privileges as a quid pro quo for extending support.'

'It's a very long shot. I doubt if it will work.'

'I've brought a brief for you to read. If you think the plan is feasible, we can discuss it further, but if you don't, we will restrict our future meetings to dining and gossiping,' Sujal said with a small smile as he passed Mazhar the note.

Silence descended as Mazhar read through it.

'It's not a bad idea to hit Jamaat and teach them a lesson,' Mazhar said thoughtfully, looking up from the paper. 'It was Sahib who gave them political legitimacy, but look at their treachery. They paid him back by joining hands with

the Nationalists to force him out of power and treat him shabbily.'

'I am aware of that.'

'Do you really believe that attacking a few Jamaat posts will help restore Sahib's position and dignity?' asked Mazhar, the doubt clear in his voice.

'As I mentioned before, our violent action is bound to have a cascading effect on the political situation. With the country plunged into chaos, the Nationalists may even be forced to call for fresh elections. Should that happen, Sahib will be freed, as both the mainstream political parties, the League and the Nationalist Party, will be desperate to seek his support in contesting the elections to get the seats required to form the government. So, it's a win-win situation for Sahib. I do agree that it is a long shot, but we must give it a try for his sake,' Sujal urged.

'What do you want me to do?' Mazhar enquired, knowing that his friend rarely did things for others without a price.

'I need 10 per cent of what Sahib promised me years ago,' Sujal said with a straight face.

'But that will still be a huge sum,' Mazhar exclaimed. 'Why can't your Agency provide the money? Has it gone bankrupt? And what about your fair-weather friends in Dhaka whom you pay regularly? Can't the League spare some money out of your regular donations to them for this purpose? Is Jamaat not their number one enemy? And, if there is a complete breakdown of the rule of law, are they not going to benefit more than Sahib?'

'I am not here to talk about others. There are reasons why I did not go to the Agency or others for money. Suffice

it to say that for this kind of operation, only your money can be camouflaged and appropriately regulated.'

'Is your chief aware that you are asking us for money?' Mazhar asked.

'No. I have not discussed this plan with anyone. This is my operation. My goal is to teach Jamaat a lesson and fulfil a promise that I made to Sahib seven years ago,' Sujal said.

After a thoughtful pause, Mazhar asked, 'Can I keep this brief? I want Sahib to read it. It may help him in taking a decision on the funding. What do I tell him if he insists on meeting you to clarify his doubts?'

'Unfortunately, that is not feasible. I cannot travel incognito to Dhaka to meet him when he is under twenty-four-hour surveillance. He has to trust me just one more time,' Sujal responded.

'Whom will the amount be delivered to and where?' Mazhar asked.

'The funds will be handled by you and handed over in Bangladesh in local currency to persons whom I will identify in due course. I will also need to know, in advance, the complete profile of the man who will deliver the payments,' Sujal said.

'You may have to think of another arrangement. It is not safe for my man to hand over money in Dhaka, particularly to locals,' Mazhar pointed out. 'If your agents turn hostile or greedy, they may have my man arrested and coerce him into identifying me as the actual provider of the funds. They can even hold me to ransom when you are no longer around.'

'It won't happen. I am going to introduce two cut-outs between you and the final recipient to ensure that no one knows where the funds come from, or to whom they

ultimately go. We will first do a test run with a smaller amount and if it goes well, only then will you start sending bigger sums. Neither one of us will be physically involved. I will explain the drill in detail once Sahib agrees to my request,' Sujal clarified.

Seemingly satisfied with Sujal's assurances, Mazhar nodded. 'Very well. I'll revert to you once I get Sahib's response.'

'Thank you.' Sujal was relieved that Mazhar had not shut the plan down before even taking it to Sahib. He glanced at his watch. 'It's late,' he said as he stood up.

Mazhar walked him out to the gate and the two men shook hands warmly before Sujal hailed a taxi and left. When he reached home it was 1.10 a.m. and still raining heavily.

The next two weeks were quiet. Reddy did not call Sujal again to ask when he was going to submit the revised proposal. None of his assets in Dhaka contacted him, either to update him on any new developments, or to ask why they had not received the go-ahead from him yet. There was also no news from Mazhar on Sahib's reaction to his proposal. Sujal remained unfazed, however. He knew that such lulls were an inevitable part of intelligence operations. Indeed patience, rather than action, was often the key to success.

The silence was eventually broken by Reddy. Although he was not the one whom Sujal was most anxious to hear from, he knew he could no longer avoid the conversation.

Reddy sounded unusually upbeat and relaxed.

'Sujal, I know the mission is keeping you busy, but please send me your revised plan soon. In fact, maybe you can come to Delhi to finalize the modalities of transferring funds.'

'Sir, I have been struggling to tailor the project to fit it within the amount that you had indicated,' Sujal said. 'I have even temporarily halted all mission-related activities till the issue of funding is sorted out. But my field operatives are becoming increasingly restive because of the delay. A few of them have developed cold feet and have dropped out. I am, however, trying to bring them back.'

'Why don't you attempt at least a cosmetic pruning to please Aulakh?' Reddy asked.

'Sir, I will give it one last shot over the coming weekend. And if I fail to come up with a viable alternative, I will come to Delhi to obtain your approval to bury the mission,' Sujal said.

Reddy sensed that Sujal was deliberately dragging his feet and would not accept a cut in either the scope of the mission or in its financial outlay. However, he chose not to push the matter further for the moment and to wait till the following week to see what Sujal finally delivered.

The next day dawned clear and sunny. Sujal left for the office early as Dayal had scheduled a meeting to discuss various operational and departmental issues. Soon after he took his seat, however, his cell phone vibrated. It was Mazhar. Sujal felt a shiver of anticipation as he excused himself to answer the call. Mazhar invited him to have lunch at his place. Sujal readily agreed and told him he would be there by noon.

This time, it was Mazhar who opened the door when he rang the bell.

'I received a message from Sahib only a few hours ago,' he said as they stepped into the living room.

'And?'

'His response is positive,' Mazhar said, smiling. After seating Sujal in the living room, he called for refreshments before continuing with the conversation.

'Sahib had many questions,' Mazhar began. 'He was keen to meet you, or at least speak to you on the phone so that you could clarify his doubts in person, but I told him that your visit would risk his safety and thus expose him to even more trouble. So we communicated via a messenger, who travelled back and forth with his questions and my clarifications.'

'Did he read my brief?' Sujal asked.

'Yes, but he isn't convinced that the plan will work. He finds your proposal fanciful and impractical. He thinks your fond hope that destroying a few Jamaat facilities would lead to widespread violence, forcing the Nationalist government to fall and be replaced by a friendly regime is an idea conceived in a moment of madness.'

Sujal smiled. 'Perhaps it is. What made him finally agree to my proposal?'

'I don't know. Perhaps he feels that implausible as it is, your plan at least offers a glimmer of hope. In his most recent communication to me he wrote that he was willing to trust you one last time. He also called me this morning to say that he was actually taking a blind chance.'

'Didn't you tell him that more than ensuring his release, my objective is to teach Jamaat a lesson for betraying their godfather?' Sujal enquired.

'I did, but he did not find this line of argument believable. He knows you well enough to understand that you are

planning something big and that the operation against Jamaat is just a smokescreen. Your real purpose, he believes, is to use the violence to put the League back in power.'

Sujal laughed. 'Sahib is crediting me for feats that I am not capable of achieving,' he said.

'Perhaps.' Mazhar smiled. 'Only time will tell. Meanwhile, he has asked me to extend all possible assistance to you in executing your task. Frankly, I was surprised at his complete change in attitude after initially dismissing your idea,' Mazhar said.

'How much has he agreed to send?'

'As much as you require. The funds will be made available whenever and wherever you need,' Mazhar assured him.

Sujal felt a surge of gratitude and enormous relief. 'I cannot tell you how much this means,' Sujal said softly, choked with emotion. 'I will let you know soon how much I require.'

'Sahib has one condition, however. If you fail to secure his release, you will have to pay back every taka,' Mazhar said, darting Sujal a mischievous smile.

'He has my word. If I have to, I will sell off all my property to repay his debt,' Sujal assured him as he got up to leave.

Mazhar looked at him seriously for a moment before responding. 'I believe you will,' he said softly. 'Come, join me for lunch. I insist.'

'No, I have to get back to the office for a meeting. But I will be in touch again soon,' Sujal said in parting.

The truth was that he was so excited at the turn of events that he wanted to rush home to share the news with Arpita over lunch. As he waited for a taxi, he invited Mazhar to have lunch with him the next day at the Taj Bengal to celebrate the faith that Sahib had reposed in him.

'Let your mission be over. Who knows, in the end, we may not have anything to cheer about,' Mazhar remarked sombrely.

'With Sahib on our side, I don't see how I can fail,' Sujal said.

On his way home, Sujal decided that he would tell the Chief that he had reached out to Sahib for funds. Once the Chief knew of Sahib's critical role in ensuring that the mission continued, he would have reason to use his resources to help Sahib's return from political wilderness.

Over lunch, he gave Arpita a full account of his conversation with Mazhar.

'Look at the irony of the situation. I am going to run an operation using funds from someone who had once threatened me with dire consequences for collaborating with the League to ensure his defeat in the parliamentary election,' Sujal remarked.

'It does not surprise me. You never had permanent enemies or friends. They were all your pawns,' Arpita said, smiling.

The Chief and Reddy looked at each other in disbelief after Sujal finished briefing them on his unusual funding arrangements. They didn't know whether to order him to stop this madness, or to go along with his dangerous, albeit innovative, plan of raising money from a shifty and opportunistic leader. The Chief wondered whether it was really possible to motivate a national leader to finance operations against his own people. Also, as far as he knew, the Agency had never conducted operations using money obtained from private sources. Every Agency officer would first submit a request for service money for a

planned operation, often even before the operational plan was fully detailed and assets to execute the operation had been identified. As the number of sources recruited and cultivated for intelligence operations grew, the demand for service money also grew exponentially, but not always for honest reasons. Despite the Agency's rigorous audit regime, the line between the reimbursement claims submitted by officers for legitimate operational expenses and money spent on their personal use was becoming blurred. As such, given the craving for service money and potential for its misuse, it wasn't surprising that the Chief viewed Sujal's proposal to procure funds from unauthorized sources with a certain degree of scepticism.

'I don't believe that Sahib will give you the money for this operation, but I am hesitant to brush aside your claim. It is incredible that you even thought of this,' the Chief remarked. 'It is an audacious and risky plan, and I will keenly watch to see how you will make it possible. I have a feeling you will not disappoint me. You have my blessings.'

Sujal could hardly believe his ears and couldn't stop the smile from breaking out across his face.

'Sir, apart from the money, your main worry has always been whether the execution of the operation could be kept secret. I assure you that the moment I sense that the mission is getting out of hand or there is any danger of our involvement being exposed, I will abort it. I won't let the Agency get a beating because of my foolhardiness. Also, not one person involved in this mission is either an Indian national or has ever been our source,' Sujal explained in an effort to address any concerns that the Chief might have over his plan of action.

'I am confident you won't embarrass us. You can run the operation on your terms. But how are you going to keep your part of the bargain to ensure that Sahib is politically rehabilitated?'

'Sir, I am working on a plan to make it happen. I may need your help at a later stage.'

'Keep Reddy updated. I may have a surprise for you when this is all over,' he said.

As they walked back to Reddy's office, he enquired if Sujal had ever undertaken an operation with money raised from such unorthodox sources.

'No, sir. Actually, funding has rarely been an issue in conducting my operations,' he said. 'However, there were occasions when headquarters would not sanction the service money or sanction less than required. I still went ahead by manipulating payments internally.'

'It is a dangerous streak in you. Unless you want to ruin your career, you should follow the advice of your seniors, work within the guidelines and avoid arguing if they disapprove of a particular course of action,' Reddy counselled.

'Sir, I generally obey orders, but when I find that there are extraneous reasons for not approving an operation or there is unwarranted hesitation in taking a decision, I push. I have indeed suffered a lot, but that's the way I work,' Sujal explained.

'Why do you have this death wish?' asked Reddy.

'Maybe the wrong officers trained me.' Sujal smiled. 'Mr Jeevnathan was one of them. He would always encourage me and push me to go boldly after targets without worrying about the consequences.'

'Well, I must say that I was quite surprised by Aulakh's reaction. I didn't think he would approve of involving Sahib in the operation, but you managed to convince him,' Reddy remarked, as he opened the door to his office. 'Wait for me. I have things to attend to, but I insist on taking you out for lunch today. We have a lot to celebrate.'

Events moved smoothly thereafter. A day after his return from Delhi, Sujal met Mazhar and requested twenty-four lakhs and twenty thousand taka. Within hours, Mazhar informed him that the money had been arranged. Soon after, Nurul came to his house to give him the particulars and address of the carrier.

'I hope the man you send to collect the money can be trusted? I must warn you that I have had terrible experiences working with middlemen; they don't hesitate to siphon off money in such covert transactions,' Nurul said.

'Don't worry. My man can be trusted. I've worked with him before and he has never cheated me or let me down,' Sujal assured him.

Later that evening, Sujal called Anisur, one of his most reliable couriers from his Dhaka days. He was surprised to hear from Sujal after so many years.

'I moved to Calcutta recently and I need your help once again. Call me on this number from a PCO in an hour. It's urgent,' Sujal said and disconnects the line.

Five minutes before the scheduled time, Anisur called.

'Please note down a number. BG7—'

'Sir, please wait. Let me get a pen and paper,' Anisur said. There was silence for a few seconds and then he asked Sujal to repeat the number.

'BG70154. This will be your identity code. Make a call to 28467853. Introduce yourself as BG70154 to the man who answers. Ask for his identification. If he says it is wxq54y, set up a meeting with him. He will give you twenty-four lakhs and twenty thousand taka,' Sujal instructed him.

'What will I do with this huge amount? I don't like the idea of keeping so much in the house.'

'Within two to four hours of your confirming its receipt to me, two persons will call you separately on your residence number to set up meetings with you. They will identify themselves as Emon and Jafrin. You will give four lakhs to Emon and twenty to Jafrin. The remaining twenty thousand is for you to buy fish and daily provisions for your family.'

'How do I contact you if the arrangements run into problems?'

'This is not the first time you are disbursing funds to my friends,' Sujal reminded him. 'I'm sure you will be able to handle any situation that arises. Now, repeat the instructions.'

Anisur went over the details without making any mistakes.

The following evening at nine, Nurul contacted Sujal to confirm that the money had been handed over to his man. Soon after, he received word from Anisur that the money was indeed in his possession. After dinner, Sujal walked across the road to the public booth and called Aziz.

'You are to call this number and identify yourself as Emon,' he instructed him, giving him Anisur's number. 'The man who answers will tell you when and where to meet him. He will give you four lakh taka. Pay three lakhs to those who provided the information on the locations of

the Jamaat camps and keep a lakh for yourself.' Sujal told him before hanging up.

Next, he called Mansoor and explained the drill to him as well. 'He will pay you twenty lakhs, which you should distribute equally among your nine volunteers,' Sujal said. 'I will send more money in due course.'

By the following evening, both Aziz and Mansoor reported that they had received the money.

Things were moving ahead again and Sujal was excited at the prospect of the impending action. But there was one more thing he had to do before he could tell Mansoor to move his volunteers to the locations to launch the assault.

Sujal summoned Israr, who took a week to reach Calcutta through clandestine routes. Both spent hours finalizing the targets from among the list of facilities and camps provided by Aziz. Israr sought some changes in the original plan.

'If we target only Jamaat's facilities along the border, they will immediately assume that the Agency has orchestrated the attacks. This will give Jamaat an excuse to call upon its cadre to retaliate. They will no doubt burn down Hindu settlements in Bangladesh, forcing Hindus to flee to India as refugees.'

Sujal listened intently, nodding. 'What do you suggest?'

'You will achieve nothing by fighting Jamaat alone. You have to create conditions in which Jamaat suspects the League's involvement in the violence and subsequently attacks them. If that happens, the League is bound to retaliate with equal ferocity, making your task easier.'

'And how do we achieve that?'

'It would be better if the assaults were directed at camps and offices located deep inside Bangladesh, so that the League activists are blamed,' Israr advised.

'What you say makes sense,' Sujal agreed.

'Since you have only nine volunteers to carry out the attacks, you shouldn't waste your resources targeting insignificant madrases and staging posts,' Israr elaborated. 'Their critical units are located far away from the border and those are the camps where armed training is imparted, propaganda material against India is prepared and contact with ISI's India-bound terrorists routinely takes place. Hit those.'

'But I want the Jamaat to get a clear message that we are punishing them for their hostile activities,' Sujal pointed out.

'They will suspect you in any case. But attacking a few madrasas and launching posts is tactically not a good idea. You must strike where it hurts most.'

'What precisely is your suggestion?' Sujal asked.

'Ideally, we should recruit more volunteers so that more targets are hit for a decisive impact,' Israr said.

Sujal went over the list of targets once again, discussing with Israr the importance and feasibility of hitting each of them. Eventually, fourteen targets were shortlisted, nine along the border and five deeper inside Bangladeshi territory.

The targets selected, Sujal told Israr that a man going by the name of Jafrin would soon meet him in Dhaka to receive the final list of targets. 'Don't ask him too many questions,' he warned. 'He is a very private person and does not like to make conversation with those he doesn't know. Just pass on the list and forget you ever met him.'

The following day, Sujal called Mansoor, aka Jafrin, and instructed him to meet Israr to obtain a list of fourteen targets. 'Call him on 29151872 and introduce yourself as Jafrin,' he said.

'Is this man reliable?' Mansoor enquired.

'He is, but a bit talkative, unlike you. He may ask you about your boys and probe you for information on your relationship with me. Parry his queries by giving misleading information,' Sujal advised.

'Why did you select a man who is so indiscreet?' asked Mansoor.

'He is very resourceful and has never failed me. Call me on the number that I gave you between 8.00 and 9.00 p.m. after you get the list,' Sujal said and hung up.

Two days later, Mansoor reported back to Sujal from Khulna. 'The meeting went well. He didn't ask any questions, just handed over the list of targets. He only told me that the number of targets had been increased to fourteen.'

'Will it be possible for you to recruit additional volunteers at this stage?' Sujal asked.

'When I read through the list, I realized that several of the targets are located close to each other. Some of the hit teams should be able to cover more than one target. So we need to recruit only three more men, which should be easy.'

'I leave the final decision to you. The time has come to let your boys know the targets they are to hit. If anyone feels jittery, drop him. Tell the volunteers that someone carrying a laminated card with the number 4pYrX4 and the symbol of a half-moon will provide them with the apples,' Sujal explained.

'But you earlier gave me a card with the same identifiers and told me that I am to use it to introduce myself to a person and collect the apples from him. I don't think the boys will be willing to talk to a stranger.'

'I was only trying to create a firewall for your safety. I didn't want the apple supplier to know you. I would rather have Shaukat and the volunteers compromised than lose my finest operational asset,' Sujal said.

'It's very kind of you to say that, but doesn't this Shaukat know who you are?' Mansoor asked.

'He doesn't. Anyway, if you are confident of handling the distribution without exposing your real identity, I have no problem,' Sujal said.

'Then let me handle the volunteers,' Mansoor suggested.

'That's fine with me. I'll call you tomorrow at 2.30 p.m. to confirm whether all your boys are on board,' Sujal said and hung up.

The next day, Mansoor confirmed that all were willing to go ahead with the mission.

'That's good news,' Sujal said. 'Now, since you want to handle the distribution of the apples yourself, the next step is for you to meet Shaukat, the supplier. He is in Dhaka at the moment. He's staying in Hotel 71, room number 215. The address is 47, Bijoy Nagar. You will have to use a different code to meet him. He has misplaced the laminated card. Do not ring him up. Go and meet him as Jafrin and give him a hundred-taka note with a serial number ending in 0250 to prove that you are the right person. Set up a secure means of communicating with each other. When the time comes, he will call you to collect the apples. You can then send them to the various venues for their sale,' he instructed Mansoor.

'Okay.'

'After the apples are consumed, your boys must maintain strict silence and avoid contacting you for a minimum of three weeks. I will be arranging for at least twenty-one lakhs, which I will send to you before the apples are sold, through the same courier I used earlier. Someone will call you after the sale to fix a date and place to give you the balance amount. If that does not happen, call me.'

'Have you fixed a date when the apples are to be sold?'

'Not yet, but I will let you know at least a week before the sale,' Sujal said and hung up.

A few hours later, he called Shaukat, who was to arrange for the explosives, and told him that a person would soon be contacting him to hand over forty lakhs. He would identify himself as BG70154.

'But our deal was that you would pay the full amount before the apples were loaded in the truck,' Shaukat argued.

'The balance will be paid on the day of the final delivery along with your commission of five lakhs,' Sujal said.

Pleased at the generous commission Sujal had promised him, Shaukat agreed to the payment terms. 'The suppliers have procured the apples and are ready to hand over the consignment. They only have to be paid. I have also rented a godown for a few days to store the apples. But who will remove the apples from the godown and load them in the truck?'

'Pack the apples into crates when you store them. A man called Jafrin will soon meet you in the hotel. As proof that he is the right man, he will now present a hundred-taka note with a serial number ending in 0250.'

'I am sorry for misplacing the card.'

'Not to worry. Finalize with him how you both will communicate with each other. And, if you have the time

and feel confident that you are not being watched, show him the godown from where he will collect the material. As soon as the apples are ready and crated, give Jafrin a call. He will take three days to lift the entire stock.'

'When can I expect to receive the advance and the balance of fifty lakhs, including my commission?'

'Don't be impatient. Please confirm first that the full load of apples has been delivered,' Sujal said tersely before hanging up.

The next person he contacted was Anisur. 'I have another job for you,' Sujal told his most trusted courier. 'It is much more lucrative than your previous assignment.'

'What do I have to do?'

'This time, you will collect money from Samuel Cleric, staying in room 207 in Sonargaon hotel,' Sujal said.

'How will I recognize him?'

'He likes wearing jeans and white polo shirts. Introduce yourself to him as Moni and show him the ID with the number BG70154.'

'When do I have to meet him?'

'Wait for my call,' Sujal said.

The following day, he instructed one of his Calcutta-based contacts, Bhuwan, aka Cleric, to fly to Dhaka and check into room number 207 in Hotel Sonargaon, where a booking had already been made in Cleric's name. He told Bhuwan that someone wearing black trousers and a grey shirt would deliver a sum of money, which he was to later hand over to one Moni, who would be carrying an ID with the number BG70154. He was to check out of the hotel immediately after the transaction was completed.

The last person he spoke to was Mazhar. He requested him to arrange for the transfer of 1,34,40,000 taka

immediately to Cleric, who would be staying in room 207 of Hotel Sonargaon.

'I can understand the bulk, but why the forty thousand? Mazhar asked.

'That's the courier's fee.'

'Why are you using another person to collect the amount? Did you suspect Anisur of siphoning off part of the payment?'

'No, but I haven't been able to contact him and can no longer delay the commencement of the plan,' Sujal lied. Actually, he didn't want Mazhar's courier to observe a pattern in transferring money.

'How will my man recognize Cleric?' Mazhar asked.

'Your courier should go to his hotel room wearing black trousers and a grey shirt. Cleric will be waiting for him.'

For Sujal, it had been a maddening week, checking every small detail of the plan's execution and leaving nothing to last-minute course correction. Finally, when all loose ends were neatly tied and all assets were primed and ready to play their respective roles, he had nothing to do but anxiously wait for Mazhar to confirm that the money had been handed over to Cleric. Once the amount changed hands, he knew the chain of events would start unfolding in quick succession. To relieve the pressure of the nerve-racking wait, he immersed himself in regular departmental work. He would drop in to Dayal's room to exchange updates on political developments in Bangladesh and discuss the unit's routine operations. He spent hours catching up with his long-neglected paperwork and remained largely confined to his room, attending to normal source work. Observing

this unexpected change in his deputy's attitude to work, Dayal asked him whether Reddy's operation had been concluded. Sujal confided, albeit impishly, that it had never taken off and had to be dropped eventually.

Arpita was not fooled by Sujal's theatrics. She sensed that her husband was close to executing the final stages of the mission. She knew that whenever he planned something big, he contrived to appear normal to calm his nerves.

The mission, however, ran into unforeseen problems. Two days after Mazhar was scheduled to deliver the money to Cleric, he received a call from him late at night.

'Did it go well?' Sujal asked anxiously.

'No.'

'What happened?'

'Cleric never checked into hotel Sonargaon. My courier tried for two days to contact him, but he had to beat a hasty retreat when the hotel management started getting suspicious and asked him why he was so desperately looking for someone who had not checked in and threatened to report the matter to the police. He had no choice but to return without delivering the amount.'

The plan seemed to be falling apart. Panic set in, compelling Sujal to take an unprecedented operational risk. The following morning, he called Israr at his home from his office line. He gave him the address of Hotel Sonargaon and asked him to contact a Samuel J. Cleric, staying in room number 207. Israr was to check whether Samuel had checked in and if he had, he was to instruct him to contact Sujal immediately in Calcutta.

When Israr insisted on knowing more about Samuel, Sujal cut him off and hung up.

To make matters worse, Shaukat called Sujal that same evening at his home number (which Sujal had given him for use in dire emergencies only) to complain that the suppliers were insisting on immediate payment and were threatening to terminate the contract if the consignment of apples was not lifted within forty-eight hours. He also wanted to know how long he would have to wait for Jafrin to come to the hotel.

'Don't worry. Give me a few hours to look into it. Meanwhile, enjoy the hotel food and relax,' Sujal snapped and disconnected the call, preventing Shaukat from giving away any more incriminatory information on an open line.

Minutes later, Vishwanath Reddy called from Delhi. He asked how the plan was proceeding and whether Sujal could come to Delhi to update him the following week. Keen to get Reddy off his back, Sujal said that the mission was on course and hung up quickly, pretending that he was having difficulty in hearing clearly due to a bad connection.

Baffled at the turn of events, Sujal decided to pay Mazhar a visit. He reached his house around 7.30 p.m., only to find that he was not there. His caretaker, however, received him warmly and insisted that he make himself comfortable in the living room.

'Do you know where Mazhar has gone and when he is likely to return?' Sujal asked, trying to conceal his impatience.

'He didn't tell me, but I know where he generally goes in the evening. He is a lonely man and spends his spare time with a girlfriend. I can give you the number,' the caretaker said with a glint of mischief in his eyes.

Sujal thanked him and promptly called the number. A lady answered and told him that Mazhar had left an hour ago for his home.

Frustrated once again, Sujal decided to try contacting Cleric. He dialled his number, but there was no response. It was only on his ninth attempt that Cleric finally answered his phone.

'I am sorry, I was in the bathroom,' he said.

'Where have you been?' Sujal snapped. 'The delivery boy has been looking for you in the hotel for the last forty-eight hours.'

'I am very much in Hotel Sonargaon, but not in room 207. It wasn't available. Some mix-up with the reservations. But why didn't he call me before he came? I would have given him the correct room number.'

'Can they deliver today?' Sujal asked.

'Yes, they can deliver it before 9.00 a.m. tomorrow. My room number is the same as the first three digits of your birthday.'

'Keep two lakhs with you and wait for my instructions. Pass the rest on to Moni. He will have an ID with the number BG70154,' Sujal said tersely and put the receiver down. He slumped back into the sofa, feeling immensely relieved.

Finally, at 11.30 p.m., Mazhar returned. Sujal informed him of the turn in events and his conversation with Cleric. They quickly went out to a PCO, from where Mazhar contacted his man in Dhaka and gave him the necessary instructions. Sujal then called Israr and told him there was no longer any need for him to look for Cleric since he had been traced.

As they walked back to the house, he admitted to Mazhar that he had used his residence phone to contact Cleric.

'You should not have done that,' Mazhar said, clearly unhappy over his friend's indiscretion. 'Please don't make the mistake of underestimating the NSI.'

'I am truly sorry, I know it was operationally imprudent, but at that point of time I was in a bit of a panic; my only thought was to get to the bottom of what had happened,' Sujal apologized. 'But don't worry. I will have your number changed within a couple of days.'

The mission was back on track. Soon after Mazhar reported that the full amount had been delivered, Sujal got in touch with Anisur and directed him to contact Cleric immediately.

'Show him the ID with the number BG70154 so he knows you're the right man. He will then tell you where and when to meet him to collect the amount. Of the money collected, you are to give eighty lakhs to Israr, twenty-four lakhs to Jafrin (Mansoor) and six lakhs to Emon (Aziz). The remaining forty thousand is your service fee,' Sujal explained the drill to him.

'Who is Israr?' Anisur asked.

'He is a friend of mine and needs money urgently for his wife's treatment in Bangkok. Talk to him on 29113426, introduce yourself as Mukul and set up a mutually convenient time and place for delivering the amount,' Sujal explained. Anisur agreed to do the needful.

In the evening, Sujal contacted Mansoor and told him that someone would pay him twenty-four lakhs shortly and asked him to get ready to collect the apples and hand over

the crates to the retailers. Sujal hinted that the sale must begin within forty-eight hours of someone informing him that the 'moon has been sighted'.

The following day he called Israr, explained the drill of receiving money from 'Mukul' (Anisur) and instructed him to promptly pass it on to one Shaukat who was staying in room number 215 in Hotel 71 at 47, Bijoy Nagar. 'Carry a half-cut apple and show it to Shaukat to establish your identity. Do not reveal your name and avoid chit-chatting,' Sujal warned.

Then he spoke to Shaukat. 'I have asked a friend to pay you the full amount within a couple of days,' he said curtly, still peeved with the agent's threat to cancel the deal if payments were not made in full or on time. 'He will contact you soon. It wasn't easy arranging all of it so quickly, but since your suppliers were insistent, I decided to pay all of it at once, rather than in instalments,' he added.

Shaukat thanked him profusely and promised to deliver the apples on time.

Sujal waited for six days, giving his assets time to receive the money, procure the explosives and dispatch them to the volunteers. On the seventh day, he contacted the owner of the PCO booth that Mansoor typically used and asked for Mansoor so that he could give him the go-ahead to commence the action. But he was told that Mansoor had gone to Jessore and would not be back for a month. Sujal realized that Mansoor probably no longer trusted the PCO owner and had therefore lied to him about his whereabouts, because Jessore was the one place that he would have no interest in visiting. He also recalled that Mansoor had shared with him his suspicion that perhaps the PCO owner was helping the watchers of the special branch to listen in on

Mansoor's conversations. But Sujal was not unduly worried. He knew Mansoor was a mature and cautious field agent, who would never put a foot wrong. Sujal guessed that he must be busy organizing the collection and distribution of the explosives, ensuring that all the volunteers reached their designated locations and instructing them on how to execute their allotted tasks. Nonetheless, now that he had no way of getting in touch with Mansoor, the question that kept bothering him was when would Mansoor launch the assault? Would he wait for someone to inform him about the sighting of the moon or would he choose the date and time on his own to mount the offensive? Knowing Mansoor's ability to adapt to changing circumstances and his sense of secrecy, it was unlikely that he would either delay the action or ring up Sujal for help in solving any unexpected problem that cropped up during the execution of the task.

Thirty-six hours passed but Sujal had heard nothing from any of his assets. The only call that came was from Israr, who told him that he had delivered the money to Shaukat. Sujal assumed that with the money paid, the rest of the plan must have been set in motion. At 9.00 p.m., while he was watching the news on television, his cell phone vibrated. Surprisingly, the caller was neither Cleric nor Anisur but Shariful Hossain. Hossain informed him that Crescent had called him the previous night from Riyadh and had told him to let Sujal know that Jamaat had agreed to gradually dissolve its relationship with the Nationalists and lend issue-based support to the League. Crescent, however, sought five to ten years to work around the majority of the cadre to break its ties completely with Jamaat-e-Islam of Pakistan.

'What did he have to say about snapping ties with ISI and refraining from pushing terrorists and radicalizing illegal immigrants in India?' Sujal enquired.

'I did ask him, knowing that you would certainly repeat this charge. He reiterated that these were wild allegations and had no basis. In fact, he suspected that you were deliberately raising these non-issues only to keep the League happy.'

'It is evident he does not want to address our key security concerns. If you think it is necessary, I can have the evidence of Jamaat's complicity sent over to him,' Sujal said.

'Both of you obviously have a serious difference of perception regarding Jamaat's agenda against India, but I still suggest that you grab this window of opportunity offered by Crescent. I sense a major shift in his stand on dealing with India and your Agency, in particular. His commitment to break away from the Nationalists is a major concession to you. Who knows, he may even temper his cosiness with the ISI in due course,' Shariful argued.

Sujal promised that he would request the Chief to seriously consider Crescent's offer and revert soon with his response.

In the long term, it made sense to accept Crescent's offer, although there was no guarantee that the Jamaat hawks would accept it or remain true to his word. On the other hand, if Sujal went ahead with the mission, any chance of persuading Jamaat to give up its anti-India stance would be lost forever. Unfortunately, Crescent's overture was too late in coming. Huge sums had already been invested in the operation, explosives had been procured and volunteers had moved out to their locations. Since his assets had gone silent, Sujal was not even sure if he would be able to contact anyone to call off the mission at this late hour

without giving away the plan to the National Security Intelligence. He eventually decided that there was nothing he could do at this point but wait and watch and deal with any consequences as they arose.

The following morning, Sujal woke up early and went out for a walk. When he returned, he found Nurul waiting for him. He had come to seek his help in getting his Bangladeshi maid released from jail for overstaying her visa. Sujal avoided enquiring if he had any news of violence in Bangladesh, for he was not sure whether Mazhar had kept him in the picture about the mission's objective. He spoke to a police officer and got the matter resolved. After Nurul left, he phoned Dayal to let him know that he wouldn't be able to come in to the office as he was running a high fever.

'Why did you lie to stay at home?' Arpita asked.

'The mission has entered its most critical phase. I want to stay at home in case anyone calls with an update. In any case, I don't want to attend Dayal's meetings on a Saturday,' Sujal explained.

He spent the day relaxing and waiting for some news but heard nothing. At 11.15 p.m., the PCO owner from across the road came to tell him that he was shutting down the shop and going home. Sujal paid him five hundred rupees to stay, in case any calls came for him. After that he retired to his bedroom but couldn't sleep. An hour later, he got up and went to the living room, fixed a small drink for himself and sat in his easy chair. His mind was racing, trying to assess and guess what was going on in Bangladesh. At 2.30 a.m., exhausted by the futility of all his guesswork, he returned to the bedroom and lay down. Arpita was fast

asleep. Just as he was about to doze off, his cell phone rang. It was Israr on the line, sounding alarmed. He said that he had tried to contact Jafrin (aka Mansoor) on the numbers given by him but they all turned out to be bogus.

'Why did you try to call him?' asked a worried Sujal.

'I wanted to know if he had been able to identify the locations that I showed him on the map,' Israr replied.

Sujal realized that Israr, who was always very curious about every detail of the mission, having heard nothing from Sujal for several days, had decided to take matters into his own hands and call Mansoor to fish for information. Annoyed, he demanded, 'Are you waking me up at this hour only to inform me that his telephone numbers are non-existent?'

'Well, no, that's not all. I was told in the evening that a clash between Jamaat and League activists took place in Bagerhat in which two persons were killed and one of them was Jafrin,' Israr said.

Sujal chided him for making unnecessary inquiries and advised him not to call anyone till he was specifically directed to do so.

At 4.00 a.m., he was woken up again, this time by a call from Mazhar. 'I am sorry to wake you up at this unearthly hour, but I believe the situation is bad there,' he said.

'Do you have any details?'

'No. I contacted a few of my people, but they weren't able to tell me much about the law and order situation in Dhaka.'

With bits of news indicating that the mission had gone more or less according to plan, Sujal felt more relaxed and slept well.

The following day being a Sunday, the Calcutta office was closed. However, Sujal decided to go in anyway to make a few discreet calls to his friends to check on the situation in Bangladesh. Since it was a holiday, only a skeleton staff was at work, manning the essential services, which suited him. Once he settled down in his room, he rang up Parimal Basu, his contact in the *Anand Bazar Patrika*, but Parimal was not in yet. Sujal then asked for the assistant editor and introduced himself when he came on the line, asking if he had any news of violence against the minority Hindu community in Dhaka. The assistant editor reported that there was no news yet of any widespread communal clashes in Bangladesh. Sujal thanked him and hung up.

Next, Sujal headed for the first floor to check the news coming in on the teleprinter. He asked the operator to show him the PTI, UNI and Reuter tickers received since last night. The operator opened a carton that was lying unattended in a corner behind the shredding machine, took out bundles of tickers and handed them over to Sujal, who sat down at a desk and began going through them. A PTI news bulletin from Dhaka filed at 8.35 a.m. caught his attention. In a series of bomb explosions carried out between 1.00 a.m. and 4.30 a.m., several Jamaat madrasas located along the border and their facilities in the Satkhira, Khulna, Chittagong, Rajshahi and Jessore districts had been severely damaged. An ISI safe house at Mujibnagar in Dhaka had also been bombed, damaging a car and killing its driver. Sujal removed the relevant ticker and walked out with it. He went to the adjoining room to check if there was any encrypted cable addressed to him. There was one from Reddy who wanted him to come to Delhi before the coming weekend. As he was about to leave, another operator

said that he had deciphered a cable from Dhaka that might be of some interest to him. It was actually addressed to the Bangladesh desk at headquarters and marked routinely to the Calcutta office for information, he said. It confirmed what the PTI had reported and provided a few more details on the damages. He returned the cable to the operator, demonstrating no obvious interest in its contents. After that, he left the office, driving home in his personal car.

From the news that was beginning to filter in, it seemed that the mission had been accomplished as planned. Though the Jamaat facilities had been hit badly and its inmates had sustained injuries, the attacks had not caused major clashes between Jamaat and League volunteers nor had there been a backlash against Hindus, as feared by the Chief. Sujal's main interest was in finding out the details of how his agents had played out their parts, but he knew that he would have to wait for at least three weeks before they started contacting him. Nonetheless, he knew enough to sense that he had delivered and a feeling of relief swept over him.

When he got home, he parked the car and rang the bell. As Arpita opened the door, he told her that he had succeeded again.

'Shariful called on your cell phone several times,' she told him as they settled down in the living room.

'He must have called to convey his sense of betrayal by an Indian friend. He would have felt that for my sake he managed to persuade Crescent to accept most of my conditions, but here I was, attacking his facilities and refusing to reciprocate his offer,' Sujal told his wife.

The Aftermath

Sujal landed in Delhi a week later. Receiving him warmly, Vishwanath Reddy said that he was proud to have reposed his faith in him.

'Sujal, although the mission went as planned, for me, personally, it is not important whether its successful execution will slow down the waves of illegal immigrants or the entry of militants from Bangladesh.' Sujal looked a little surprised as Reddy continued, 'What matters the most to me is that it has given me an immense sense of belief in the ability of some of the Agency's officers to pull off such a difficult operation with only moral support from the leadership. Well done.' He smiled.

'Sir, I'm not sure what to say,' Sujal responded, overwhelmed at Reddy's warm words.

'No need to say anything. Your actions have spoken far louder than any words could have. Now, let's go meet the Chief. He's been waiting to receive the jewel of his crown.'

As they entered Aulakh's office, he stood up and came around his desk to embrace Sujal. 'Congratulations, Sujal. It is a rare accomplishment for any officer to execute a mission with zero cost to the Agency. It is definitely the first of its kind in my entire career,' the Chief enthused. 'Although no reward can match your deed, still, as a token of our appreciation, I have approved your assignment to a European station.'

'Sir, thank you, this means a lot,' Sujal said.

'You've earned this. Now you will neither have to borrow money to run operations nor work under interfering officers,' Aulakh reassured him. 'Reddy, I want you to

recommend Sujal for the Agency's highest operational honour.'

Not accustomed to hearing such praise, Sujal simply thanked the Chief for his generous words. As they walked back to his room, Reddy confided to Sujal that he had already initiated the paperwork to transfer him from Calcutta to headquarters.

Back in Calcutta, Sujal was in high spirits. He couldn't wait to share the news of his assignment to a European desk with Arpita. However, he had a few things to take care of before he could start packing and planning for his next assignment.

The first thing he did was to meet Mazhar and request him to make an additional twenty-five lakhs available to reward the boys for executing the mission. Although Sahib initially refused, saying that he had agreed to pay for the mission and not for rewarding crooks, Sujal's promise to help ensure his political rehabilitation eventually swayed him and he agreed to release the money. With the money secured, Sujal's final task was to make arrangements for it to be collected and distributed amongst the boys. He called Aminul Islam, a businessman and one of his all-weather contacts in Dhaka, and told him that one Mustafizur would contact him the following week to hand over sixteen lakh taka. This was to be distributed among five individuals who would approach him shortly with slips notifying the amount. He excluded Israr from the list of beneficiaries of the reward because Shaukat had complained that instead of the promised eighty lakh taka, he had received only seventy-eight lakhs. Sujal was convinced that Israr had siphoned off the two lakhs.

With the loose ends all tied, Sujal left Calcutta to join headquarters, unaware of the misfortunes that were awaiting him.

The first to go after him was Dayal. Although he had tolerated Sujal while he was posted in Calcutta, knowing that he didn't have much choice in the matter as he was running an operation for Reddy, Dayal wasted little time in trying to put Sujal in his place after the latter was transferred to headquarters.

Dayal wrote a letter of complaint to Jaspreet, his immediate senior officer at headquarters, alleging that Sujal had kept him in the dark on most of his operations. He requested Jaspreet to find out whether Sujal had indeed been authorized by Reddy to run an operation independently because Sujal had informed him that Reddy's operation had been abandoned. He alleged that Sujal had used his posting in Calcutta to float businesses in the name of his family members with the help of his Bangladeshi sources and friends.

Jaspreet was convinced by Dayal's accusations and decided to get to the bottom of what had happened. He confronted Sujal with the allegations.

'I am not authorized to speak about Mr Reddy's operations,' Sujal said. 'As for my business interests, they are a private matter and I will not discuss them,' he added.

Fuming at the brush-off, Jaspreet met both the Chief and Reddy. They paid no heed to his complaints and accusations. To mollify Jaspreet, however, the Chief advised Sujal to file a report highlighting the operation's purpose as cultivating Jamaat's top leadership, but leaving out the violent aspect of the plan, names of assets and the source of funding.

Jaspreet found the report insulting and went after Sujal with renewed vigour. This was helped by his chance discovery of an outline of the plan in Vijay's computer. Dayal added fuel to the fire by informing Jaspreet that one of his assets claimed that Sujal had paid lakhs to mysterious travellers from Bangladesh and that Saumen Das, a junior field officer in the Calcutta office, had arranged for their escort and accommodation. A cable from the Agency's station chief in Dhaka further confirmed Jaspreet's suspicion. It quoted one of his assets as claiming that Sujal had spent crores on an operation but had paid nothing to one Israr, who was made to sign a receipt for five lakh taka for working as Sujal's courier. When Jaspreet reported this to Reddy, the latter advised him not to carry out an autopsy on a dead mule. Jaspreet's meeting with the Chief was even more frustrating. The Chief heard him out patiently and then enquired about his ailing wife. Once again, his efforts to uncover the 'truth' didn't get him very far.

Jaspreet was convinced that the Chief and Reddy had invested hugely in the operation, which had been horribly botched, and the trio was busy covering up their dirty tracks.

Things changed for worse when the Chief retired and Reddy was transferred out of the Agency. With Sujal's supporters no longer in the picture, Jaspreet resumed his inquisition. The first thing he did was to visit Dhaka, but he was unable to find any incriminating evidence. The source who had referred to Israr's claims did not come forward for questioning. Jaspreet was also unable to find any records on Israr either in Dhaka or in headquarters. The man existed nowhere.

Still, he refused to give up. He summoned Sujal again.

'I have evidence that you ran a bogus operation, pocketed huge sums of service money by underpaying sources and later destroyed the accounts of all transactions. The choice before you now is to either seek voluntary retirement or be dismissed from the service on security grounds,' he threatened.

'What are you waiting for?' Sujal countered. 'I know what evidence you are referring to. I can also line up hundreds of witnesses to manufacture evidence.' He stormed out of the room.

Infuriated by Sujal's intransigence, Jaspreet briefed the new Chief about a fake operation that Sujal had run in collusion with 'an operationally naive' Reddy and alleged that the officer had misappropriated a huge amount of service money to float several businesses under bogus names. The Chief promised to look into it and, if needed, order a departmental inquiry against the officer. True to his word, the Chief summoned Sujal and asked for a detailed briefing on the Jamaat operation. At the end of it, the Chief remarked that the operation sounded more like fiction, as he found it hard to believe that anyone would fund an operation to kill his own countrymen.

'If you think I am weaving a tale, I can arrange for you to meet Mazhar in Calcutta,' Sujal said.

A week later, on Sujal's advice, the Chief travelled to Calcutta to meet Mazhar. Amazed at what he heard and realizing that Sujal had indeed managed to pull off a unique operation, the Chief asked Sujal to submit a full account of the mission to him. This he put in his archive along with the Agency's other untold success stories and rewarded Sujal by clearing his posting to a European station that had been approved by his predecessor.

Jaspreet's parting shot was to record in Sujal's annual confidential report that he had a tendency to misuse government funds, fudge reports and run bogus operations. When it was sent to Reddy to review, he tore the adverse remarks apart and gave Sujal a thumping chit. The Chief agreed with Reddy.

Four years later, Dayal, who had by now moved up the ladder in the Agency's hierarchy, refused to give up his witch-hunt. He consistently gave Sujal poor performance assessments and blacklisted him for future foreign assignments. By this time, Jeevnathan had returned to headquarters. Jeev listened to his protégé's travails and was amazed at how he had managed to retain his fighting spirit, his eagerness to launch challenging operations and his zest to work for the nation's good. Although it was too late to repair the damage to Sujal's career, he did what he could to make the leadership realize why Sujal was different from other officers. He was also able to get the embargo on his foreign assignments removed.

Sujal Rath bore the indignities he suffered well and seldom betrayed his pain. He refused to resign or seek voluntary retirement even when his juniors were promoted over him, some even serving as his bosses. He once told Jeevnathan that he wanted to test his mental strength to see if he could overcome falsehoods and continue serving as he saw fit. He did not let the politics of his senior officers affect his morale and continued to conduct operations on his own terms, contacting and meeting his overseas sources and political friends without informing the Agency. He used one of them to get Sahib rehabilitated and thus kept his promise to Mazhar. Never shy of reaching out to his foes, he revived his contact with Shariful Hossain and Crescent and

tried very hard to save the latter from being incarcerated, but the League would not agree to Crescent's freedom. They eventually hanged him.

Sujal Rath has since retired. However, politics in Bangladesh remains his abiding passion. Defying the Agency's norms that prohibit officers from maintaining contacts with assets after leaving the office, he regularly meets and communicates with his Bangladeshi assets.